An
Infinite
Number
of
Monkeys

For Leila—

Here's to Monkey Business!

Best,

[signature]

1991

An
Infinite
Number
of
Monkeys

Les Roberts

St. Martin's Press
New York

Design by Jessica Winer

Library of Congress Cataloging in Publication Data

Roberts, Les.
   An infinite number of monkeys.

   "A Thomas Dunne book."
   I. Title.
PS3568.O2389I5   1987   813'.54   87-4402
ISBN 0-312-00610-1

First Edition
10 9 8 7 6 5 4 3 2 1

To friends and lovers
who helped me tough it out.

An
Infinite
Number
of
Monkeys

o 1 o

My *Ficus benjamina* was dying. There wasn't much I could do about it except sit there listening to Stan Getz records and watch it die. I had watered it, fed it plant food, given it lots of light and even talked to it, but nothing seemed to help. I couldn't bring myself to throw it in the garbage, not while there was still some life left. The plant was not unlike my just-ended relationship. We'd known it was dying and tried all sorts of things to save it, but we didn't throw it away until it was completely dead. And now she was gone, Leila was gone, and I was watching my ficus die. I finished up my third cup of Lapsang souchong tea, and it tasted like shit. That's the trouble with Lapsang souchong. The first cup is sensational, dark and smoky with an afterbite that gets you toward the back of your throat. By the third cup it is as though a heavy cigar smoker has been using your teapot for an ashtray.

The ringing of the telephone was an intrusion on my death-watch. I was going through a period of existential angst, wondering what to do with the rest of my life, and I didn't want to talk to anyone. But I thought it might be Leila, calling to beg me to take her back. I had no intention of doing so, not after so many weeks, but that was still one phone call I didn't want to miss. I picked up after the fourth ring.

"Thank God you're home. I need you." It was Jo Zeidler, my office assistant and my friend, and the strain and ragged anxiety in her small voice made the short hairs on the backs of my hands prickle.

"What's wrong, honey?"

"Someone just tried to kill Marsh. Can you come over?"

I was reaching for the stereo off switch as I said, "On my way."

It was raining hard, a common December occurrence in Los Angeles, drumming on the rag top of my Fiat, drowning out all but

1

the highest treble notes on my tape player as I drove from my place in Pacific Palisades to the Zeidler apartment in West Hollywood. The street's surface shone like a reflecting pool and it was difficult to make out the white lines on the street that kept traffic from becoming total anarchy. Combined with the impeded visibility that even my wipers couldn't cut through, it made for a slow and careful drive, and by the time I parked in front of the palm-festooned apartment building south of Santa Monica Boulevard my eyes were smarting from the strain.

When Jo had made sure of my identity through the fish-eye peephole in the door, she let me in and almost fell into my arms, and with my hands on her back I felt the sob she was trying to stifle. I smoothed the black hair back from her damp forehead and she led me into the living room where Marsh, her husband, was huddled on the sofa in what was almost a fetal position. He blinked owlishly through his New York Intellectual glasses and managed a weak smile.

Jo was the dearest friend I had, a cute and energetic lady with the common sense of an Earth Mother and the fierce loyalty of a Doberman pinscher. She was more friend and confidante than bookkeeper and secretary, and there were two good reasons we had never become lovers. The first was that it would have severely damaged our wonderful friendship, and the second was that she was very much in love with her husband. Marsh Zeidler was a transplanted Easterner who, like me, had trekked West to make his mark in the film world. But where I had wanted to be an actor, Marsh's ambition was to write the Great American Screenplay. I had achieved some modest success and Marsh had found none at all, so I stayed solvent between acting jobs by running my own seat-of-the-pants investigative agency, and Marsh paid his rent waiting on tables at a trendy crêpeteria in Westwood. He was a sweet and ineffectual man of thirty who looked forty-five and had the emotional maturity of fifteen, and he was a nebbish and a nerd to boot, but for reasons not readily discernible to me Jo loved him, and that made him aces in my book. I couldn't think why anyone would want to kill him unless he'd put his thumb in their onion soup fondue.

His voice was even reedier than usual when he spoke, and it

quavered like a six-year-old's who was trying not to cry. "Some guy took a shot at me from a car," he said.

"Are you sure it was a guy? Did you see him?"

"No. When I heard the shot and the bullet went by my head I just hit the dirt. The mud—it was raining like hell. I didn't see anything."

"Make of car? Color? License?"

"It was too dark out. A big, dark car." He shrugged apologetically as though the dearth of information was his fault. That was typical Marsh—he seemed to be asking the world's pardon for being here.

"What did the police say?"

He looked away. "I didn't call them."

"Why the hell not?"

"Buck said not to."

Jo anticipated my next question. "Remember I told you Marsh was doing some writing with Buck Weldon?"

I nodded. Buck Weldon had been one of the best-selling authors in the 1950s with a series of whodunits about a ridiculously tough and macho private eye named Bart Steele and his escapades with busty overblown blondes and sadistic and oversized triggermen and Communists and Mafiosi. The mixture of gut-wrenching violence and crude graphic sex had made Weldon a millionaire, and even though his reputation had faded as the times had grown more free and frank, his ham-handed style was still much imitated and his titles still outsold the work of newer and more skilled authors. Marsh had gotten an idée fixe about turning one of Weldon's more recent efforts into a feature film, and for some inexplicable reason the aging writer had agreed to make a stab at a screenplay collaboration.

"Buck Weldon was here when it happened?"

Marsh said, "I was out at his place in the Valley. We'd been working a few hours and he ran out of bourbon. He seemed to be coming down with a cold—he's got a chronic sniffle anyway—and it was raining and I offered to go to the liquor store. He's got this iron gate in front and I was just opening it when the car drove by. The bullet hit that brick, uh, column the gate hooks onto, about two feet from my head. I saw the muzzle flash."

"Rifle or handgun?"

"I don't know. I don't know anything about guns. I went back inside and Buck said to forget it. He said not to call the cops because they only gum things up anyway." He glanced up at Jo. "Only he didn't say 'gum.'" It was typical of Marsh, too, not to want to say "fuck" in front of his wife. God knows she'd heard the word before—she worked with me.

"Marsh," I said patiently, "Buck Weldon is living in his own novels, not reality. Now, can you think of anyone who might want to hurt you? No matter how farfetched? An irate customer, a writing competitor, a . . ." I looked at Jo, not wanting to say "lover." Finally, I didn't. It was too absurd to suggest anyway.

"Who'd want to kill me?" Marsh whined. He was on the thin edge of hysteria. "I'm only a waiter."

"Did you mention to anyone, even casually, that you were going to Weldon's house tonight?"

"No. I don't like to talk about my work until it's finished," he said, which meant that he didn't much talk about his work at all. "Jo was the only one who knew."

"Might Weldon have told anyone?"

"I wouldn't think so. Only his daughter. She lives there with him, she's his secretary."

"Would she have any reason to shoot you?"

He laughed in spite of himself. "No—she was in the house when it happened."

I glanced at my watch. It was just past nine. "Marsh, the police have to be called."

"No, please don't. Buck won't like it."

"Fuck Buck," I said, immediately aware of the absurdity. I turned to Jo, usually the voice of reason, but she gave me no backup.

"If Mr. Weldon gets angry it may spoil Marsh's chances of working with him," she pleaded. "This could be Marsh's big break."

"Marsh can't work with him with a bullet in his head, Jo." Her eyes were supplicating, and it was shaking me. "I don't know what you want me to do, Jo. Hand-holding is your department." That came out more harsh than I'd intended, but that's the way it goes sometimes.

4

"Maybe," she said in a small voice that I found irresistible, "if you could talk to Mr. Weldon so he wouldn't be mad at Marsh—maybe then we could call the police."

"Somebody tried to kill your husband!" I said angrily. "No movie deal is worth that. I don't understand you!" But I did. I understood all too well the desperation to make good in an industry where the briefest scintilla of time can make the difference between fortune and accolades and prestige and clout and a table at Ma Maison, and anonymity and poverty and the vinegar taste of failure. I'd been there at one time myself, I'd played the games and kissed the asses and fawned and curried favor until one morning I'd gone to my mirror to shave and found there was no one looking back at me, and that's when I opened my agency, Saxon Investigations, and after that I almost didn't give a damn about acting any more except as a well-paying hobby.

Marsh was huddled on the sofa as though awaiting chastisement, and Jo stood with her arms hugging her small breasts and swaying slightly as if the wind of adversity was buffeting her almost off her feet. They were two people about whom I cared very much, and at this stage of my life there were certainly precious few of them around, and I knew that I would become involved here even though my better judgment told me to go home and turn Stan Getz over and spoon some more PlantLife into my terminal ficus. So I sighed and told Jo to get Buck Weldon on the phone for me, too late remembering we were in her home and not at the office. She didn't seem to mind, though, and in a moment handed me the receiver.

"Hey, Saxon, I've seen you in movies," came the raspy, familiar voice, New Jersey in origin and sandpapered with untold shots of bourbon and countless unfiltered cigarettes, with the warmth of a genuinely decent man. "What can I do for you?"

"I'm sorry to bother you this late, Mr. Weldon."

"Buck," he corrected. "Don't sweat about the time, I'm night people."

"Then you wouldn't mind if I came to see you?"

A slight pause. "Now?"

"It's about what happened to Marsh tonight."

"Yeah. Well, okay, sure. Can you stop off and get some Wild Turkey on the way?"

I got the directions to his house in the Valley and hung up, then turned to Jo, half-ignoring Marsh in the manner of a school teacher talking in the presence of a first-grader to his parents on Open House night. "You can't just let people shoot at you and do nothing. That's what we pay the cops for. I'm telling Weldon that I'm going to call Joe DiMattia in the morning." I took her upper arms in my hands and kissed her chastely on the mouth. "Don't come to work tomorrow. Stay here with Marsh, keep the door locked and don't let anyone in but me. I'll call you later." I left them there, Marsh still on the sofa and Jo behind him, her hand on his shoulder, a formal Victorian family portrait of terror.

There is no logical way to get from West Hollywood to Verdant Hills in the western San Fernando Valley, perhaps because the city planners couldn't conceive of anyone ever wanting to. I chose a twisting two-lane through the hills called Beverly Glen, and in the heavy rain my Fiat labored like a determined salmon swimming uphill to the spawning grounds. The Glen wound past the lavish estates north of Sunset Boulevard until they gave way to the quaint rustics of the canyon dwellers, and then near Mulholland Drive at the top of the Santa Monica Mountains the homes became high-priced ranch moderns for the newly wealthy. As the road began its descent into the Valley these new homes were replaced by the dreary sameness of suburbia.

The San Fernando Valley had gained its fame via a popular song of the forties that extolled the virtues of its country pleasures. In the forty years since, it had metamorphosed into an overbuilt, smoggy, crowded community of nearly three million souls who lived as stepchildren to the rest of Los Angeles for the illusion of living in the suburbs. In reality they lived in unimaginative tract homes and condos and "swingle" apartment complexes, the poor devils. Why Buck Weldon chose to live in a place so contrary to his tough image I couldn't figure. But then I couldn't figure why anyone chose to live there. The Valley makes my teeth ache.

Weldon's house wasn't hard to find, even in the rain. It was on a medium-size street, its iron gates and brick posts just as Marsh had described them. I made a U-turn and parked at the curb, then walked through the downpour to the gate, stopping to examine the bullet gouge in the brick. I went up the driveway to the house and, grateful to be protected from the elements by the overhang of the porch, I rang the doorbell.

Buck Weldon himself came to the door. I was shocked at how short he was, no more than five foot six, but the broad shoulders and muscular neck made him seem bigger. Still, even from my not-exactly-towering just under six feet I could see where his brush cut was thinned on top. I knew he was close to sixty but he looked much younger, and his handshake was that of a man in his vigorous prime. He noticed my empty hands.

"Where's my Wild Turkey?" he said.

"Oh, shit, I forgot it. I'm sorry."

"Doesn't matter, doesn't matter. Come on in out of the rain, for Christ's sake."

He led me through his living room, with its gadgety stereo and animal-skin rugs, and into his study. It was a totally masculine room, done in rich woods and leathers, with a suitably cluttered desk, and IBM Selectric II with a half-typed page in its roller, and a whole wall of books that looked well read, unlike those bought by people because their dust jackets matched the drapes. There was a deck of Bicycle playing cards on the desk that had been quickly pushed together and not evened out. Buck sat behind the desk and gestured me into a club chair, hacked a heavy smoker's cough and sniffled. His nostrils were red, and there was a box of pop-up tissues at his right hand.

"Want a beer?" he said. "I don't drink it, even though I sell it on TV. Gives me gas."

"Thanks, but I'm wet and cold already."

"Coffee then? To warm you up?" He bellowed "Tori!" and then sat back without waiting for an answer, looking me over with frank curiosity as though cataloguing me for future use as a character in a book. Then he said, "Whatsisname, Marsh, he's told me a lot about you. You act and you're a private eye, right?"

"Private eye is Bart Steele, Mr. Weldon. I'm an investigator."

He waved his hand in front of his face, a gesture that I was to learn was one of his favorites. "You can call yourself a vestal virgin for all I care. Marsh says you're a hell of a guy. Thinks you walk on water."

"In this weather you have to."

He laughed, nodded, appraised some more. Then, "You ever read my stuff?"

"Sure. Hasn't everybody?"

"Whaddya think?"

"I'm not a literary critic—"

"You think it's shit." It wasn't a question.

"Come on, now! I think it's great entertainment."

"So's a blow job but that doesn't make it art. That's okay, I've got no illusions. They say you can take an infinite number of monkeys and sit them down at an infinite number of typewriters, eventually one of them will write *Hamlet* or something. So this old monkey writes books about Bart Steele. It's a living." He squinted at me through cigarette smoke. "Like acting."

"Don't take it out on actors because Hollywood has ruined a couple of your books."

"Hollywood didn't ruin my books," he said, and pointed a thick finger. "They're right up there on the shelf."

I relaxed in the warmth of the leather chair. "It's still early to say, Mr. Weldon, but I think I'm going to like you."

"Then call me Buck, I already told you."

We both looked up as the door opened, and I got to my feet as gracefully as the overstuffed chair would permit, and stood there staring at the woman who had just come in, feeling like a tourist gawking at the Great Sphinx, except she was even more spectacular than that. I didn't dare move. I felt as though someone had pulled out the little cotter pins that kept my leg bones connected to my thigh bones, and my knees almost knocked. She wasn't tall, perhaps five foot four, but she moved with the grace of a much taller long-legged woman. Her eyes were an impossible, unbelievable green with an iridescent blue undercast to them, and were set wide apart beneath her broad forehead. Her cheekbones were classically sculptured, worthy of either of the Hepburn ladies, and her mouth was full and almost pouty and begged to be kissed and nibbled and caressed, and her blond hair had a just-tossed look that made me want to put my face in it and leave it there for a long time. Yet there was a sadness about her, a sort of bruised and aching look that for me added to the overwhelming sensuality of one of the most striking women I'd ever seen in my life. Her look was not inviting; just the opposite, it said she'd been hurt a lot and please keep your distance. It wasn't that she looked as if she'd been crying; instead it seemed she'd cried so much that there were no tears left.

"This is my daughter Tori," Buck said, and she turned those green eyes on me and smiled a kind of three-quarter smile, and I felt like I'd grabbed a high-voltage wire.

I tried to think of something dazzling and impressive to say. I managed to croak out, "Hi." One of my better bon mots.

"Tori's my secretary, my confidante, my good right arm," Buck said with paternal pride. "I don't know what I'd do without her."

I was wondering what *I* was going to do without her. I said, "Miss Weldon—"

"Tori, for God's sake. You're a formal bastard, Saxon," Buck said.

"Tori . . . you were here when the shooting occurred?"

She nodded. "I was reading in my room. It was raining pretty hard, and you know how loud that gets. And I was playing music—Duke Ellington."

Score another one for her side, I thought.

"So when I heard the shot, I didn't really know what it was. I mean, I've never heard a shot before except in the movies."

"And then what?"

She knitted her beautiful brows for a bit. "When Marsh came back in the house Dad came and knocked on my door and I came out. That's the first time I realized what had happened."

"You didn't see a car?"

"It must have been long gone by then . . . I didn't even look."

Buck said, "It was just a bunch of punks, that's all."

She looked up at him, her eyes flashing. "I don't think so, Dad. This isn't that kind of neighborhood."

"You don't think they're going to shoot up their own turf, do you? Honey, Mr. Saxon wants some coffee."

She turned to me again and I got lost in her eyes. "How do you take it, Mr. Saxon."

"Black," I said. I'd almost answered blond. I suddenly didn't want any coffee any more because that meant she'd have to leave the room to get it.

"Good," she said. "I think you'll like my coffee."

I knew I would. I didn't take my eyes off her until the door closed behind her. I couldn't remember the last time a woman had made such an impact on me.

Buck said, "Don't make too much of this business, Saxon. A bunch of kids get high on something and go around shooting off Saturday night specials, that's all."

"Shooting at someone's head isn't exactly a school prank."

"Maybe not when I was a kid, or you, either. But times have changed. They don't upend trash cans any more, or soap windows or drag-race on Mulholland Drive. Now they drive around and shoot off guns. It's a rite of passage." He stubbed out his cigarette and immediately lighted another, coughing and sniffling at the first puff. "We've come a long way from the malt shop."

"You'll have a tough time convincing Marsh that getting shot is the capper to a high school pep rally."

"Who'd want to kill Marsh, anyway? The man is a walking apology for living."

"Then why are you writing with him?"

Buck squirmed around as if trying to mold his butt to his chair. "Well, the kid came to me with an idea, and he was so goddamned earnest, and I thought I could control him so that when the picture did get made it would bear some slight resemblance to what I wrote in the first place. Plus he's a nice kid—plus plus—he thinks I'm a terrific writer. But I guess the real reason is my writer's block."

"Come again?"

"I'm having trouble with my new book—getting out of a plot hole I wrote myself into. I've been blocked for a month. So I thought if I took a few weeks and worked with the kid on the movie it would break the logjam and get me back on track." He peered at me. "Now you think I'm a bastard. A user."

It somehow touched me that this wealthy and famous man cared about my personal opinion of him. I shook my head. "Not at all, we all use each other. That's what makes the world turn. Besides, you're doing Marsh a favor."

10

He seemed relaxed now, exonerated. "Too bad he got shook up tonight, but tell him it's okay."

"I'm sorry, Buck, but I don't see any guarantees of that."

"Figure it out, man, the kid's a waiter in Westwood. He's got about seventeen bucks in the bank, he wouldn't say shit if he had a mouthful, and the last time he put his pecker someplace it didn't belong was in 1971. My God, if he jaywalks on a lonely street he turns himself in and falls on the mercy of the court. Hardly a candidate for premeditated murder. It was just one of those episodes of random urban violence, that's all."

"Anyone you know that might not want a film made of that particular book?"

"Twenty million moviegoers. They've stayed away from the others in such numbers you'd think they were organized." He sniffed a big sniff again.

"No one else?"

"Everybody else stands to make money. My agent, my publisher, my ex-wife, my daughters—"

"Daughters plural?"

"Victoria—Tori, you just met her—and Valerie. They each get five percent of my income off the top. I set it up so they could enjoy my money while they're still young and while I'm still alive." The pitch of his voice dropped appreciably and there was a hard edge to his tone. "I don't want anyone doing happy handsprings when I die."

"Are you planning on dying sometime soon?" He looked up, bellicose, and I went on, "You're a man who spends his life writing about killing and dying. I just wondered if you think about it a lot."

He quoted, "'It seems to me most strange that man should fear; seeing that death, a necessary end, will come when it will come.'" He smiled smugly. "Shakespeare."

I countered, "*Julius Caesar,* Act Two, Scene Two. Caesar to Calpurnia."

"Okay, I'll stop showing off if you will."

"Deal."

Tori Weldon came back in with the coffee. This time I was prepared; this time I wasn't taken by surprise. This time I had a devastatingly witty, charming, Cary Grant-style remark all ready. "Thank you," I said.

"You're very welcome." I tried to interpret all sorts of hidden meanings into the "very." I succeeded. My knee was literally quivering when she handed me the steaming mug. I was staring a lot harder than I should have been, and she noticed it, and she didn't exactly blush, because there was no false coyness in her, but she did lower her eyes quickly. I felt guilty that I'd made her uncomfortable and wanted to spend the rest of my life making it up to her.

"Are you investigating this business in an official capacity?" she said.

"No—I'm just a friend of Marsh's. His wife works for me."

"Oh," she said, nodding. "Well, if I can help you in any way—"

"I'll be in touch."

"Good," she said. I watched her when she went out—the rear view was among the best I'd ever seen—and I looked at the door a little too long after she'd closed it behind her, and Buck caught me looking and grinned.

"She's something, isn't she?"

"I'm sorry, Buck, I didn't mean—"

"Hey, she's a beautiful woman. I don't blame you. But she's kind of vulnerable right now. Take it easy."

"How vulnerable?"

"Forget it," he said. "She's a great kid. Got her mother's looks and my brains, thank God. Her sister Valerie only got the looks."

"Does Valerie live here too?"

"No, she's got an apartment near UCLA."

"What does she do?"

"She's studying to be an artist. But what she does mostly is smoke pot, put out for colored guys, and ask her old man for money. She's eighteen going on forty—my late-in-life baby. Two minutes of pleasure and eighteen years of *tsuris*."

"And Tori?"

"Tori's older. She was married once, but she moved back in with me a little over a year ago. Right after her divorce. Used to be married to Deke James—he was a wide receiver with the Chargers." I never heard anyone manage to convey so much dislike in such a few innocuous words. I guessed that Deke James was one of the reasons Tori Weldon walked around like an exposed nerve.

"Buck," I said, changing course, "I still don't know what to tell Marsh Zeidler. It's hard to buy a story about joyriding Valley Boys."

"Buy it, rent it, take it back for a refund," he said cheerfully, "that's probably the *emmes*."

"Then why not notify the police?"

He spread his hands helplessly. "Look, I'm a public figure. The books, the TV commercials, the talk shows. If the cops come, the press comes, my face is all over the six-o'clock news, and all sorts of shit comes down on me."

"Such as?"

"Such as—my beer sponsor, which pays me two hundred biggies a year to sell their mule's piss to rednecks, decides it's bad for their image to have their spokesman involved in Crime." The capital *C* was in his voice, I just record it here for accuracy. "Such as—the cops start hanging around here to protect me and my reading public thinks the tough, mean badass who writes Bart Steele needs help wiping his own tush and they start buying Mickey Spillane books instead. And such as—some looney-bird hears about it and goes out to buy his own Saturday night special to gun down the right-wing fascist who writes books glorifying vigilantism. And for what? The cops aren't going to do a damn thing except tell you it was a bunch of kids high on lid poppers."

I took a gulp of coffee. It was good, with the flavor of chicory, strong as though it had been on the warmer a while. "You missed your calling, Buck. You should have been a trial lawyer."

"Has the jury reached a verdict?"

"Sorry, but I'm going to have to call Joe DiMattia at LAPD in the morning. He'll keep it quiet."

"He a buddy of yours?"

"As a matter of fact he hates my guts. But he's a good, fair cop and I'll explain how you feel about the publicity. He'll take it from there."

He rubbed a hand over his eyes and nose, and all at once he looked his age. "I don't suppose I can talk you out of it."

"Sorry."

"Okay—I see your point. But I'm telling you nobody wants Marshall Zeidler dead."

"Let's hope you're right."

"You're a pretty good friend of his?"

"His wife is my assistant and my friend. I love her. She loves him. *I* love him."

"Is that how it works?"

"For me."

He stood up. "You're not a bad guy for an actor."

"Easy, Buck, I can't handle effusive praise."

"Hey, have you read my latest book?"

"Uh—*The Avenging Angel*?"

"That's my publisher's title. I think it sucks."

"What did you want to call it?"

"I'm lousy with titles. They can call it *The Maltese Falcon* as long as they send the checks." We went to the bookcase and he took down a copy and began autographing it for me. "So you won't give it away to the library book drive."

I looked at some of the other titles on his crowded shelves. He owned the complete works of Hammett and Chandler, most of Ross Macdonald, Bill Pronzini, Hemingway, Steinbeck, Jack V. Kale, John O'Hara, and several books by and about Presidents Kennedy, Truman, and Theodore Roosevelt. I took down one of the Kale novels and thumbed through it.

"Read any Kale ever?" he said, scribbling on the flyleaf of *The Avenging Angel*.

"All of it, several times. He's great."

Buck grunted.

"They say no one's ever seen him. He lives in the hills in Mexico and never comes to plug his books on Donahue or Carson or pick up his Pulitzer Prizes. You'd think he'd like to get in on some of the fame."

Buck snorted, "The only thing fame ever got me was laid, and I'd like to think I could have swung that anyway. He probably cashes the checks and is a totally happy man." He shut the book and handed it to me and said, "Here—a collector's item. This and fifty cents will get you a cuppa coffee anyplace in town."

"I'm sorry about the cops, Buck. I'll make sure the lid stays on tight."

"Hey, keep in touch, huh? I like you."

"I like you too," I said. "And I hope your writer's block clears up."

He laughed. "You make it sound like a rash."

"I'll see myself out," I said. I waited a beat too long. "Please say good night to your daughter for me."

He suppressed a smile. "You've got the phone number. Call her and tell her yourself."

"I will," I promised.

I walked back through the house very slowly, hoping to catch one more glimpse of Tori Weldon before I left, to spare myself calling up the next day and saying, "Hi, you probably don't remember me but I was at your house last night—?" But she was nowhere to be found. Bitterly disappointed, I ran through the raindrops to my car, sticking the book under my raincoat to keep it safe and dry.

I let the engine warm up for a few minutes, and before I could pull away the front door opened again and a small figure came running out toward me. Tori had a scarf almost obscuring her beautiful blond hair, and a cape was tossed over her shoulders. She looked good enough to eat. She came around to the driver's side and I rolled down the window, and my throat tightened at the proximity of her.

"I need to talk to you," she said.

"Sure. Get in."

"No, not now."

"Get in, for God's sake, it's raining out there."

She hesitated a moment and then came around and got in on the passenger's side. I rolled up the window, partly to keep out the chill and partly so I could get the full impact of her perfume. It was subtle, sexy, young.

"Can we have lunch tomorrow?"

"I was planning on calling and asking you anyway."

She shook her head. "This isn't social."

"I can't tell you how disappointed I am."

"Look, I need you. It's important." She put her hand on my arm and I could feel the warmth of it through my raincoat, jacket and shirt. I could also feel the trembling.

"Tori, what's wrong?"

"There's a restaurant on Ventura Boulevard," she said, and gave me the name. We set our date for twelve-thirty.

She said, "I'm frightened. I'm more frightened than I've ever been in my life."

And she looked it. My heart went out to her.

She said, "I can't talk about it now. Meet me tomorrow." And while I watched she got out of my car and ran back into the house, head down with one hand clutching the rain cape around her neck, the other outstretched as though groping for the warm light coming from the doorway. She looked very young and very small, Goldilocks lost in the woods. I ran a hand through my hair.

I was still aching from Leila, from the pain of the ending and the leaving. The last thing I wanted was any sort of serious involvement. I had decided that once I recovered from the loss, fun and games was to be my escutcheon. But I knew, or rather sensed, that Tori Weldon was not a lady to be casually tumbled and then forgotten. I felt she couldn't take it, and I wasn't sure if I could, either. I had no idea why she wanted to lunch with me, but I had a sinking feeling it wasn't my warm, exciting little body she was after. She was in some kind of trouble, and one look into those wondrous green eyes and I was ready to supply whatever she might want or need. If I could appear as her knight in armor, her rescuer, why then, so much the better for my just and noble cause. Whatever it took, I was going to get to know Tori Weldon, and the prospect so excited me that I almost forgot about someone using Marshall Zeidler's head for target practice.

Almost.

I made it home an hour later, wet and cold and tired, and irked because my car's tape player had just eaten a favorite Dizzy Gillespie cassette. My ficus seemed to have weathered its latest crisis and was resting comfortably, if not off the critical list at least out of immediate jeopardy. I poured myself a Laphroaig Scotch neat and took it into bed with me along with my new copy of *The Avenging Angel*. On the flyleaf Buck had written: "To Saxon. Don't start acting like Bart Steele. You'll just get your ass in a sling." The signature was almost illegible but the advice seemed sound. I opened to a page at random.

> The guy was big, big like the wall of a high school gymnasium, with mean little eyes and a slack, stupid mouth, and a nose like a rutting hog. It was the nose I went for, and when my fist connected solidly it spread all over his fat face, and I felt the nose blood and mucus hot on my knuckles. His eyes crossed like he was looking for the end of his nose, only it wasn't there any more, it was mashed flat into his puss. It was one of my better rights—a sucker punch, I admit, but those were the best kind. He sat down hard, and he was out before his big ass hit the sidewalk.

And when his big ass hit the sidewalk it was time for me to get out of bed and pour myself another Laphroaig. There was no question about it, Buck Weldon wrote with his feet, but still there was a spareness, a kind of punchy, direct cadence to his writing that was not unpleasing. I could see why Marsh Zeidler thought it would make a hell of a movie.

> She let the little white panties slither the rest of the way down her long legs and stepped out of them in a way that let me know she'd done this a lot before. She was stark naked, and in the flicker of the candle her blond bush gleamed a burnished gold. Her breasts were fabulous, overripe and tanned as the rest of her, with big pink aureolas and tip-tilted nipples that hardened when the night air hit them. "See anything you like, Steele?"

Buck Weldon seemed to live in a world where all breasts were overripe melons and all pubic hair was burnished gold. All Bart Steele's women came complete with the staples in the navel. I supposed that reflected Buck's own tastes. Anyway, I wearied of the sex and the beatings after about fifty pages, and, whether I'd been thinking of her before I went to sleep or whether I was actually dreaming about her, Tori Weldon and her green eyes were there with me in my big empty bed.

I woke early the next morning, ground enough coffee for four cups and called Joe DiMattia after my second one. Lieutenant Di-Mattia had been, at one time, the hardest guy on the street. He'd gotten wide in the gut from too many of Mama DiMattia's linguine suppers and he tended to puff a little if he ran up the stairs, but he was still capable of tearing out your lung. He'd been married to a lady much younger than himself for about five years, and they had a pretty good thing going, but in her single days she'd worked as a secretary at Paramount Studios and had run around with a lot of different guys in the business. Mine was the only name on that list that DiMattia knew about, and every time he looked at me I knew what kind of pictures he was seeing in his head and it really bit him in the ass. I felt sorry for him in a way—and in a way I enjoyed it. Okay, so sometimes I'm not a very nice person.

"I didn't think you pansy movie stars got up before noon," he said when I'd identified myself. He had one of those reedy, high-pitched voices like Brando's in *The Godfather,* and if he'd decided to go crooked when he was a kid on the Buffalo streets, he'd prob-ably *be* a godfather by now.

"We don't," I told him. "The orgy with the five starlets and the German shepherd just broke up and I called to tell you night-night."

"Whaddya want, Saxon? I'm busy here."

"I want to report a shooting in Verdant Hills."

"Call West Valley Division."

"I need to talk to you, Joe."

"Why? I don't like you. Every time I see you I feel like cleaning my fingernails."

"Then we should see each other more often. Look, Joe, this hap-pened outside Buck Weldon's house—the writer. A friend of mine walked out the door and someone took a shot at him."

"Since when do you have friends?"

"He wasn't hit but he was shook up." I told him the story, in-cluding why no one had called the police. When I'd finished I

18

heard him breathing through his oft-broken nose. Then the breathing pattern changed.

"I'll tell Jamie Douglas out at West Valley to poke around very quietly," he said. "All right?"

"Thanks, Joe. I'll be your best friend."

"Fuck you, Saxon," he said, and hung up.

I had my third cup of coffee as I scanned the paper, then took my fourth one into the bathroom while I showered like a kid preparing for his first date. Tori Weldon had fallen on me like a stone wall in an earthquake, one of those magical people who come along all too rarely in your lifetime and touch you deeply in spots you didn't even know you had. Aside from her startling beauty, for after all there are a lot of beautiful women out there, more so in Los Angeles than anywhere else, I was well aware of what Tori's appeal was. I have always managed to get myself involved with women who were emotionally needy, maybe because of my own need to feel like a knight in shining armor. Put me in a room with fifty gorgeous women and I will unerringly seek out the little bird with the broken wing, take her in and nurse her back to full health. Unfortunately it most often happens that as soon as their wings heal, they fly away into the sunshine.

I arrived at the Encino restaurant a few minutes early. The bar didn't stock single-malt Scotch, and I hated house wine, so I had a Perrier and waited. Tori was an on-time person, too—she arrived at twelve-thirty-two, dazzling in a white angora sweater with a boat neck and padded shoulders, and a wide flowered peasant skirt with knee-high brown boots, and her hair fluffed loosely in the back and pulled up over her right ear. Once again I was aware of the impact, ganglia aquiver.

She declined a drink, making me glad I hadn't ordered one. She seemed nervous and tense, but wouldn't talk about it until the waiter had taken our order.

"I have some good news for you first," she said.

"The good news is that you're here," I told her. "Everything else is an anticlimax."

"Please," she said, and I, unable to deny her anything right now, desisted. "The good news is that you needn't worry about your friend Marsh. No one wants to hurt him."

"You could fool me. I saw the bullet mark."

She said, "Marsh had been at the house since afternoon, since before it started raining. He had no raincoat or hat, so when he offered to go to the liquor store Dad loaned him his. Whoever it was thought they were shooting at my father. Not Marsh."

"Who would want to hurt your father?"

"That's what I want you to find out. I want to hire you."

I shifted in my chair. "Buck seems to think it was a bunch of hopped-up kids."

She shook her head impatiently. "Last week someone tried to run his car off a cliff in Malibu Canyon. They almost succeeded. The car hit a big rock and broke an axle, otherwise it would have gone over."

"It could have been an accident."

"No—he was really scared. He said someone had tried to run him off the road—to kill him. He wouldn't have admitted that unless he was scared."

"This is sounding more and more like police business."

"You know how Buck feels about that. Besides, the bullet hit the brick gatepost. If they were to find it, it would be too smashed up to trace."

I looked at her with admiration. "That's pretty good," I said.

"Don't forget, my father writes detective stories," she smiled. "I know all about ballistics and forensics and things like that."

"Tori, I don't do bodyguard work," I said. "I have a friend, Ray Tucek, that I usually use when the need arises. Maybe I could have him come out and—"

She waved the notion away in the same gesture her father used. "He'd never allow that. Pride. You see, in a way he thinks he is Bart Steele." She allowed herself a tiny, sad smile. "But Bart Steele never gets older or tired, and when he smokes his three packs a day and drinks his fifth of bourbon it never seems to bother him." She looked up at me, and I could tell she was trying not to cry. "Find out who wants to hurt my father, Mr. Saxon."

I hesitated, uncomfortable. It was hard to negotiate a price with a woman I was already half in love with. I said, "I'm expensive."

"That's unimportant."

I quoted her my fee and she brought out her checkbook and

wrote a check for a week in advance. Her checks were imprinted with sunbonneted little girls playing with balloons, and her handwriting was childish. The dots over the i's in Victoria were big round circles.

"I just can't go knocking on any door," I said, "you'll have to give me a start. Who are his friends, his enemies, the guys he bums around with . . ."

She put a hand up to her blond forelock and fluffed it absently. "He knows a lot of people . . ."

I took out pen and notebook and waited patiently.

"Jeremy Radisson," she said, finally. "He's the president of Hermes Books—Dad's publisher."

"Is it strictly business, or are they close?"

"They socialize on occasion, but they're different kinds of people. Jeremy is like a cartoon of an elegant rich man."

"Why would he want to harm Buck?"

"I don't think he would, Mr. Saxon, but you asked who Dad's associates were—"

"I'm sorry. Go on."

"Well, there's his agent, Elliot Knaepple." She pronounced it "Ka-nop-uh-lee," and spelled it when I asked her to. "Elliot was a kid just out of the mail room and Dad was an unknown writer—they started out together. Elliot is younger, of course."

"Do they have a good relationship?"

"Elliot likes anyone that makes him a lot of money. Bart Steele isn't the hot item it was ten years ago but the books still do well. Almost singlehandedly Dad has made Elliot a rich man. He can be an asshole sometimes."

The vulgarity coming out of that angelic mouth jarred badly, and I shook it off. "In what way?"

"Name it. He thinks he's God's gift to the female race." I didn't point out that females were not a race unto themselves. "And then there's Shelley Gardner."

The way she pronounced the name made me put an unobtrusive little asterisk next to it in my notebook. "Who's he?"

"She. My father's—lady."

"You don't like her much?"

"She's like one of Bart Steele's girls. All boobs and peroxide and phony eyelashes." She gave me Shelley Gardner's address, not too far from where we were at that moment. "He pays the rent," she added unnecessarily.

The waitress arrived with our food, and conversation slowed for a while as we ate. Lunch was utilitarian but a long way from three stars in the *Guide Saxon*. Then I said, "Tori, these names you've given me—they all sound like they have a vested interest in keeping your father healthy. Doesn't he have anyone who dislikes him?"

"Just the moral watchdogs of American literature."

"You mean Jerry Falwell is a suspect?" The joke was ill-conceived, and I wished I could have chased the words as soon as they left my mouth, and caught them before they reached her.

"No one really dislikes Dad," she said coldly.

I wished I had ordered a drink, because I wanted to take a big gulp of it before I said, "What about Deke James?"

Her eyes narrowed, becoming almost Oriental, but still green as Chinese jade. I knew I'd hit a raw nerve. "What *about* Deke James?"

I was sorry I'd had to bring it up. "You tell me. I got the feeling from Buck last night that he's not very fond of Deke James, and I wondered if it were mutual."

She sat rigidly, looking ahead of her, and it was instantly apparent she wasn't going to answer. Her face closed as did the subject. But I jotted Deke James's name down in my notebook.

"What about your sister, Valerie?"

Tori gave me her Westwood address. "Valerie is what used to be known as 'wild.' She's into drugs and all sorts of craziness, and she's packed a lot of living into eighteen years. Maybe once a month she'll show up at the house for dinner and a check—Dad is her sole means of support. Once in a while she'll free-lance some artwork. She's really pretty good."

"You disapprove of Valerie's lifestyle?"

"Does it matter if I do or don't?"

"No. Just trying to fit pieces together."

She took a red and white box of brown Nat Sherman cigarillos from her purse and I hastened to light one for her. She looked uneasy smoking, as if it didn't really come naturally. "Val is my sister and I love her. I don't always like her, but I do love her. Okay?"

"Okay," I said. "Now, who else? Drinking buddies, card-playing cronies? I saw cards on his desk."

"He plays solitaire while he's writing—says it clears his mind. I don't know how, but that's what he says. And he'll drink with just about anyone. Oh, wait, I did think—a professor of American literature at UCLA. He did an important thesis on Dad and they've been quite friendly over the past five years or so. Professor Bo Kullander. He's from Sweden, and Dad is part Swede himself, so they were kindred spirits from the start."

The Swedish heritage explained the cheekbones and the wide, generous mouth I was trying so hard not to stare at. She had just about finished her Caesar salad before I'd even started my London broil. She ate like a Ukrainian peasant who didn't know when next he would see another good meal. I somehow found that adorable, but then there was nothing about this woman that was not. I gave her my card and on the reverse side I scrawled my home phone number, hoping against hope she'd use it. "If you think of anything else, call me."

"There are two conditions here, Mr. Saxon," she said. "The first is that Buck isn't to know I've hired you. He'd throw us both out on our butts." I tried to visualize hers, an almost overwhelming distraction. "The second is that no one else is to know either."

"What do I tell all these people I'm going to have to talk to?"

"That's why I'm paying you," she said. "Figure it out." She dabbed at her lips with the napkin, and I envied the napkin. "Ready?" she said, and stood up without waiting for a reply.

We went out to the parking lot and I walked her to her car, still feeling sixteen. She was beautiful even in the sunlight, her pink lipstick and green eyes and blond hair and smoky eye shadow washing over me like the colors in a desert twilight. I said, "Tori—have dinner with me tonight."

I was sure a woman as beautiful as Tori was asked out a lot, but it seemed to make her tremendously ill at ease. She shook her head. "I'm sorry."

"Is there someone else? Are you involved?"

She almost laughed. "Hardly," she said.

"Well, then why not?" That was a question I never thought I'd hear myself ask.

"Not while this is going on."

"When it's over?" I pushed. "Look, I'm really lousy at game-playing, and I've got to tell you I am very smitten with you. I just want to get to know you better."

She was looking at something beyond my right shoulder as she brushed at her bangs. "I can't make any commitments. I get very frightened when I feel attracted to a man."

"We don't have to go pick out furniture. Just dinner. And no hard sell afterward."

Her green eyes bored in to my very core, questioning me and my sincerity, and then she looked away and unlocked her car door and got in, the fullness of her skirt cheating me out of a flash of thigh. "I can't really discuss it now," she said, and then added, "Please keep in touch about this other thing," and the car door's closing was a period, ending negotiations for the time being. I watched as she backed out of the parking spot and moved slowly down the lane and out of the lot, jostling over the speed bump that made her hair bounce, and then she was out on the boulevard and gone, and it wasn't until that moment that I realized, and was blown away by the fact, that she'd admitted she was attracted to me, and I was suddenly unaware of anything else, even that I was standing in the middle of the traffic aisle, until a Valley housewife in a designer pantsuit blew the horn of her enormous Cadillac for me to get the hell out of the way.

I went back into the restaurant to the pay phone in back between the two rest rooms. In keeping with the place's nautical motif the john doors were labeled CAPTAINS and MATES. Putting cutesy appellations on the doors of public toilets has always irked me, as though the words STALLIONS and FILLIES, KINGS and QUEENS, or POINTERS and SETTERS somehow obscure just what it is people go in there to do. I've always fantasized opening a seafood restaurant just so I could label the bathrooms OYSTERS and CLAMS and watch the patrons try to figure out which one they were.

I called a relieved Jo Zeidler to let her know Marsh was off the hook, and then I called Shelley Gardner, figuring that if I saw her today it would save me another trip to the Valley. Her voice was a bit fuzzy on the other end, and I could tell she'd been drinking, even though it was only just past two in the afternoon. I told her I was an actor trying to put together a film based on Buck Weldon's books and asked if I might see her to get some background. It was a pretty flimsy story, but it worked, because she asked me to come right over. Maybe she was just starved for company.

She lived on the ground floor of an expensive apartment complex in Encino, and her apartment fronted on the swimming pool. The weather being as it was, the pool area was deserted, and the gaily colored lounge chairs and umbrellas looked as if they had been quickly abandoned when the nuclear bombs started falling. In the cold, damp air the steam rose eerily from the hot water spa, and I could hear the pool filter and pump churning and gurgling and grinding. The door to Shelley Gardner's apartment was smoky green and the knob was in the middle of the door, a refinement I was sure added fifty dollars a month or so to the rental.

Shelley opened the door almost immediately. She was the embodiment of every woman Buck had ever written about. Her breasts were indeed melonlike—and at war with the white silk shirt that barely confined them. The tight green slacks held in an ample behind atop a pair of long, strong legs. She was chorine-blond and wore fresh makeup, too much of it, thick enough that if she had scratched her cheek her long red fingernails would have left furrows in the greasepaint. I wondered how she looked without it. She wasn't much older than Tori—thirty-five at the outside, but it was thirty-five the hard way. Her apartment was all white, ruffled curtains and velours and silks and exaggerated femininity. The butt-filled ashtrays were a contradiction, and the stale smell of old cigarettes almost overwhelmed that of her perfume.

She ushered me into the living room and made a stab at being a gracious hostess. "I've just opened a bottle of chenin blanc," she said. "Want to help me with it? Or would you rather do some stardust?"

Now I'm just cornball enough that when someone mentions stardust I immediately think of Hoagy Carmichael. But I'm not so stupid that I don't know stardust is slang for cocaine, and I most definitely didn't want to do any. Sometimes I drink too much, but I am very anti-narcotics, which makes me something of an anachronism in Hollywood. I said, "The wine sounds nice."

She indicated that I should sit next to her on the puffy white sofa and she poured us some wine. It was good wine, not the jug stuff found in supermarkets. "So," she said, appraising me the way an out-of-town conventioneer would look over a call girl the bell captain had sent, "you want to do a Bart Steele movie, huh? Are you going to play the part? You're cute enough—but I don't think you look tough enough."

"They do wonderful things with padding," I said, noting that Shelley Gardner needed no padding at all.

"So how can I help you?"

"Give me a little background, anything about Buck that could give me some insight into the man himself."

She looked at me through slitted eyes, one brow cocked, reinforcing my opinion that my cover story stank. She blew smoke in my face. I figured since I was going to be inhaling hers I might as well get it firsthand, and I lit a cigarette of my own.

Finally she said, "I think you're full of shit."

"Take a number."

"What you want from me is to tell you how to get around Buck so he'll give you the permission you need. You're operating out of your hat and this is your first little test run. Am I right or wrong? Say, who gave you my number, anyway?"

"I'm a little embarrassed, Miss Gardner—"

"Shelley. That's okay. I've been with Buck almost five years, and three or four times every year some sharpie tries to get to him through me."

"I don't want you to do anything except fill me in. It really would be most helpful when I finally talk to him."

She took two drags from her cigarette and a big swallow of wine before she spoke. "Why not? Why not, huh? Okay. But only 'cause you're cute. If you weren't cute I'd toss you out of here on your ass."

"I'll have to remember to thank Mom and Dad."

"The first thing is, don't talk so fancy to Buck. And don't dress so fancy, either. He's a down-to-earth guy, he likes to belch and fart and talk sports and be one of the guys. That's why he hangs out in bars a lot, getting into trouble."

"Trouble?"

"He thinks he's a badass and he gets into hassles. He generally talks his way out of them, but not always. And he's no kid any more."

I chose my words carefully. "These fights—do they ever get serious? I mean, does anyone ever get mad enough to want to get even?"

"Barflys never remember what happened the night before," she said. "It's mostly chest-thumping and muscle flexing, and once in a while they shove each other a little."

I leaned forward and refilled her wineglass before she could ask me why I wanted to know. "It must be fascinating being so close to a famous man."

She snorted. "Fascinating!" She drank down half the fresh wine I'd poured her. "Half the time he's too blitzed to do anything—you know."

I nodded. I knew.

"And those goddamn trips of his!"

"Trips?"

"Every three months or so he just takes off, disappears for a week or so. He never takes me with him. Maybe he's got something going on the side."

"Where does he go?"

"Christ knows. It's like he drops off the face of the earth or something. Writers are weird." She crinkled her nose at me in little girl fashion. "So are actors."

"When was his last trip?"

"About six weeks ago. Hey, what's going on here? What's all this got to do with your movie?"

"I'm just trying to get the feel of things."

"I'll give you a feel," she muttered, and it was almost a threat.

Her wine was gone again, and I refilled her glass, feeling not terribly admirable about doing so.

"Does Buck talk much about his work?"

"No. Sometimes he reads me stuff that he particularly likes. But they all sound the same to me—brass knuckles and big titties and the size hole a forty-five makes in your head. I don't even listen any more, you know what I'm saying?"

One of my least-favorite pieces of trendy jargon is "you know what I'm saying?" as if the speaker were addressing someone who understood only Urdu instead of a literate, well-read and witty person such as myself. In view of this I neither assured her that I knew what she was saying nor called her on it, but instead changed the subject.

"What's he writing now?"

She was holding the wineglass up to the light and rubbing at smudge marks with her finger. For a moment I thought she hadn't heard my question, but then she said, "It's about movies. Movie stars and Hollywood shit. Like I say, I don't pay much attention." She slumped against the cushions, waving the glass, almost spilling the wine, looking like the kind of girl Gloria Grahame used to play in films, the Slut with the Heart of Gold, the Rich Man's Plaything, drinking to postpone the eventual good hard look at reality. "I don't think Buck's Hollywood pals are going to like this new book much. But they won't be *mad*. They like having a writer around, they think it gives them class." She gave a short, mirthless bark. "I've seen more class in the men's room of a porno movie arcade."

"Is there anyone in particular, in the movie business, that Buck is close to?"

"Buck," she said, making an effort to speak with perfect elocution, "is buddies with the whole world." She slumped even lower in the sofa, and one nipple was peeking out between two of the beleaguered buttons on her blouse. I doubt if she was even aware of it, even though her manner was suggestive and somewhat flirtatious. I think she was just going through the motions, as though seductiveness was expected of her. "You're not asking any of the right questions," she said sullenly. "Who are you, anyway?"

"I've told you. Check me out with the Screen Actors Guild if you don't believe me. I'm a member." I stood up. "Thanks, Shelley. You've been very helpful. I might call you again."

"Anytime," she said without getting up, without even sitting up. "You call me anytime—because you're so cute."

I let myself out and walked past the steaming Jacuzzi feeling a bit put off. I didn't like being cute. High school cheerleaders are cute. Kittens and puppies are cute. And stuffed bears and four-year-olds and tennis outfits and certain very skilled welterweight boxers are cute. I wanted to be fascinating and sophisticated and darkly dangerous and an object of unbearable desire and longing. But ever since pubescence women and girls have been calling me cute. Just one of my many crosses.

I drove to a nearby cocktail lounge and drank a Glenfiddich neat to get the taste of chenin blanc off my tongue, and after two sips I went and called Tori Weldon to tell her of my meeting with Shelley.

"Why didn't you tell me about these little trips of Buck's?" I said.

"I forgot. He's been doing it for so long I just kind of take it for granted. Ever since the third Bart Steele came out and he started making a lot of money. He just announces he's leaving one day and disappears. It was kind of rough on his marriages but it never stopped him."

"Marriages?"

"My mother—mine and Val's divorced him about fourteen years ago. She died a few years after that. His second wife, Candy—they were married less than a year—is remarried and living in Camden, New Jersey."

"Bitter divorce?"

"Not at all. They just realized they'd made a mistake and they parted. He made a generous settlement on her. Even though she's remarried now she gets a piece of some of his work. You want her address in Camden?"

"Maybe later. Anything else you forgot to tell me?"

"I don't know. I don't know what's important or not."

"Everything could be important, Tori. What about the book he's writing now? Have you read it?"

"I retype it every day for him after he stops work. He's on about page one sixty-five now."

"Any chance I could read it?"

"I don't think so—he'd have a cow."

"He wouldn't have to know."

"I don't like going behind his back—"

"You went behind his back to hire me. Look, Tori, it could be very important. I'm still in the Valley. Is there any chance you could bring me the manuscript tonight? Say, at dinner?"

She gave a little exasperated half-sigh. "You don't quit, do you?"

"You wouldn't like me if I did. And I'd be a liar if I didn't say how much I'd like to see you tonight. But to be honest, I really need to read that manuscript."

We set a date at a quiet French restaurant in Sherman Oaks, and then I hung up and called my answering machine only to find no one had called me. Then I dialed the administrative offices of the San Diego Chargers some 120 miles to the south, and when I told them I was putting together a series of articles for the Hearst newspaper chain they were only too glad to give me Deke James's home phone number. When I called Deke he agreed to see me the next morning "if it won't take too long," and gave me directions to his place in Mimosa Beach. Then I made an appointment with Professor Kullander for the next afternoon at UCLA, and after that I was out of change because calling just about anywhere from the Valley was a toll call. So I had another drink and then I wandered eastward on Ventura Boulevard with lots of time to kill. I stopped off in the famous Sherman Oaks Galleria, the natural habitat of the Valley Girl, and I watched them all in their leg-warmers and designer sweatpants and spiky hairdos and the torn-looking shirts that made it seem they had recently been sexually assaulted, and then I bought a new shirt at one of the mall shops because I didn't want to have dinner with Tori Weldon wearing the same shirt I'd been in all day. To eat up two hours I saw a movie in one of the Galleria's theaters, a little number about a homicidal maniac running amok in a convent. After I changed my shirt in the theater's men's room I stopped off in the bookstore and did some heavy browsing among the cookbooks, bought three of Weldon's paperbacks that I didn't remember reading, and headed to a nearby record store where I found some Morgana King and Sue Raney records on sale among the displays for Def Leppard and Bon Jovi. Finally it was time to go, and I wandered for half an hour among the color-coded ramps and levels trying to find my car.

Tori arrived at the restaurant on time, wearing a clinging black dress that was startling in its elegant simplicity and that made her eyes look like emeralds, and when she sat down she handed me a large manila envelope. "This is a first draft," she said. "He'll most likely do one or two rewrites when the whole thing is finished. I felt like a Russian spy sneaking it out of the house."

"Siberia's nice if you're into skiing," I said. I hefted the envelope. "I really appreciate this. It might not mean anything, but if it doesn't I'll at least get a kick out of being the first one to read it besides you."

"I'm sorry to burst your bubble," she said, "but Elliot Knaepple, Dad's agent, has read the first hundred pages, and so has Jeremy Radisson."

"The publisher?"

She nodded. "He likes to know when he forks out a fifty-thousand-dollar advance that Dad is really working."

"When did they read it?"

"About three weeks ago. Jeremy was enthusiastic but he said he was worried about lawsuits."

"Why is that, Tori?"

She tapped the envelope with a fingernail. "You'll know when you read it," she said. That was a little mysterious for me, but then that's what my business is all about, so I guess I had a little mysteriousness coming to me.

"Hungry?"

"Not really after that big lunch. Usually I just eat one big meal a day. Have to watch my weight."

From where I sat there wasn't an ounce of excess flesh on her anywhere. I speculated on how much fun I would have looking for some.

"Aren't you going to read this?" she said.

"Now?"

"I can't let you keep it overnight. Buck will want it in the morning."

"I can't read it here," I said, indicating the restaurant's low, intimate lighting. "I'll go blind. Besides, it'll take me a few hours."

"Well, let's go someplace where you *can* read it," she said. "Do you live alone?"

Now, I have watched many a similar scenario fall into place in the singles haunts of Marina del Rey. I've even been party to one or two. But I couldn't believe this one was coming together this way with a woman I wanted so badly. I started to sputter, winding up sounding like Ozzie explaining to Harriet why he had been up on the roof all afternoon. She rescued me.

"You drive and I'll follow you. That way you won't have to come all the way back to the Valley.

"Tori," I said, but she held up her hand.

"I'm trusting you."

I leaned over and took that hand, the touch of her electric as ever, and I said, "I'd sound like a jerk if I told you I wasn't sexually attracted to you. That's the main reason people get together. I never heard a guy look across the room and say, 'There's a really unappetizing-looking woman, but I'll bet she's a nice person so I'll ask her to dinner.' But somehow every time I look at you my brain turns to Wheatena. You're the most beautiful woman I've seen in the past ten years and whatever I'm feeling about you is scaring the shit out of me, too."

She squeezed my hand gently and said, "I promise then I won't take advantage of your vulnerable state tonight. But if it will help Buck I want you to read that manuscript right away. Shall we?"

She stood up as I scrambled gracelessly to my feet and tried to bear up under the keen displeasure of the head waiter when he found we were leaving without ordering and he'd have to reset the entire table with fresh linen and silverware. I was intimidated enough to leave a handsome tip for no service whatever.

I jumped on the San Diego Freeway nearby, heading south, being careful at all times to keep Tori's Mustang in sight in my rearview mirror. She was a good follower, and it was only about twenty minutes later that we pulled up in front of my apartment building.

"This isn't how I pictured your place," she said.

"You expected an army cot and a cockatoo in a downtown hotel for winos?"

She laughed. "I didn't know what to expect. Are you going to offer me a drink?"

"Sure," I said, "Scotch, vodka, gin, Armagnac, red wine, white wine, Diet Pepsi, coffee, tea—"

"I think Scotch—and may I have some coffee too?"

"I drink a single-malt Scotch called Laphroaig," I said. "You take it neat."

"Sounds fine."

"I'll put the coffee on."

"You do the drinks, I'll pour the coffee," she said.

"You'll have to grind some. The beans are in the freezer—they stay fresher that way."

"I'll find everything." She went into the kitchen. I heard her opening drawers and cabinets and running water as I poured the Laphroaigs, and then I heard the whir of my little coffee mill. Morgana was singing how it feels to be lonely, something I knew a little bit about, and it gave me a jolt to realize how good it was to have a woman futzing about in my kitchen making me coffee. I held both drinks until she came back into the living room, then I gave her hers and we tinked glasses. There didn't seem to be an appropriate toast, but she knew that and smiled at me and kept those emerald eyes on me over the rim of her glass while she sipped.

"This is good," she said. "You've made a convert."

It embarrassed me, even annoyed me, that I was so tongue-tied in her presence, I who always had a quick reply for everything. But that's the effect she had on me, and that's what happens to smart-asses.

She said, "You don't have to entertain me. I'll find something to do until the coffee's ready." She gave me her father's manuscript. "Read," she ordered.

I switched on the lamp and sat in the chair I favored over all my other furniture, a rich brown-colored easy chair with a nubbly fabric that was comfortable in all weathers and temperatures, and I set down my drink next to me. I remembered my last time in this chair, about twenty-four hours earlier, drinking tea and watching my dying plant. I glanced over at it. A lot had changed in just one day—I had a case, I was a few dollars ahead, and I had met a woman who was turning me inside out just by showing up. But the ficus had not benefited from my good luck. It still drooped sadly, its leaves hanging limp and dejected in the attitude of a Little League baseball player who has struck out with the bases loaded in the last inning and his team one run behind.

She moved over to the built-in bookshelves against one wall and looked at the titles. "I see you like the classics."

"Show me a modern guy who writes like Twain or Melville and I'll love you for life." I dropped my voice. "In fact you don't even have to do that and I'll *still*—"

"I see you read Steinbeck, too—and Saul Bellow and Jack Kale." She turned and looked at me and I couldn't tell whether there was impatience or devilment in her eyes when she said, "You're not reading."

I often wear glasses for reading and for watching plays and movies. They weren't absolutely necessary but they did cut down on eyestrain a lot. But I would have died before I put them on while Tori floated soundlessly around my living room. I was already self-conscious about my premature gray hair, for the first time in my life. She stayed at the bookcase for a while, her perfume turning the apartment into a floral bower, and then she selected an anthology of American short stories and curled up on the sofa opposite me, kicking her shoes off and tucking her feet up under her, and the look at her legs that I had missed earlier in the day when she'd gotten into her car was made up to me and then some. She had the most terrific knees I'd ever seen. I tried hard not to stare at them, or at least not to get caught doing so, as I took Buck Weldon's typed manuscript out of the envelope, settled back in my chair, and began to read.

For the first fifty pages or so there were few surprises. It was pretty standard Buck Weldon fare, with Bart Steele the typical avenger-without-portfolio, smashing his way through an assortment of big hired muscle and exacting a terrible revenge along the way for the death of a movie actor pal of his, and becoming involved with one of the biggest sex goddesses in filmland.

Like every other red-blooded American boy I had fantasized about that body, lusted after it, dreamed about it awake and asleep. Norma Keene's body was the fuel for a lot of guys' jack-off reveries, and for them it was always enough, a chimera, an impossible dream like pitching in the majors or being president or winning an Oscar. But here I was, an ordinary guy, and her big breasts were like pillows in my hands and those fabulous long legs were wrapped around my shoulders. When she took me in her fabled mouth and worked me expertly I knew that dreams and fantasies really can come true, and the force of my coming seemed like it would blow off the back of her head.

It frankly embarrassed hell out of me to read that while Tori sat quietly across the room, knowing she had also read it, even retyped it. I sneaked a look at her and she sensed it and glanced up from her book and I reflected how little she resembled the fictional Norma Keene, and I was glad she was not the sexual fantasy of millions—only mine.

I read a bit further and got more into the plot and then I realized what the book was about and I knew why Jeremy Radisson was worried about lawsuits. I also knew why there might be a few people who didn't want Weldon to finish this particular book.

Everyone who reads newspapers or follows the comings and goings of the entertainment world had to be aware of the story of Sherwin Mandelker, the former film studio chief who had quietly embezzled more than $200,000 from Mercury Pictures until the well-known actor, Jeff Quinn, had caught him at it and had broken the unwritten Hollywood code about keeping one's mouth shut. Quinn had gone to the DA and to the *Los Angeles Times,* blowing the whistle as he went, and the resultant scandal had been the biggest since the Fatty Arbuckle affair. Oddly enough, the denouement was that Mandelker had left the studio and set up a successful independent production unit financed by Mercury, and that the demand for Jeff Quinn's services had mysteriously dried up. It was perceived as a de facto blacklist, a warning to all others that the first commandment of Hollywood, "Thou shalt not air the industry's dirty linen publicly," was not to be broken.

And here in Buck Weldon's manuscript, with Bart Steele running around bedding movie stars and beating up hired muscle, was the whole Mandelker-Quinn story, almost the way it had happened, with the names changed and a fictionalized studio to keep the lawyers from hyperventilating. Sherwin Mandelker was written as venal, ruthless, greedy, and unprincipled, which was pretty much the way he was. He would certainly not be pleased with his portrait.

It took me another forty-five minutes to finish, during which time Tori brought me another drink and more coffee. I carefully evened up the pages and put them back in the envelope, and then I looked up at her and said, "This stuff is murder." Certainly an ill-chosen phrase.

"No one's read it but Jeremy and Elliot. Unless they gave it to someone else."

"On that possibility alone I think someone ought to be watching Buck on a full-time basis."

"I told you, he won't allow that."

"He doesn't have to know. I mentioned Ray Tucek. He's worked with me before. He's good, discreet, and knows how to stay out of sight. It'll cost about a hundred and a quarter a day."

"It's not the money," she said, chewing on her lip. "It's just so— horrible to have a bodyguard."

"It might be more horrible not to," I said. I called Ray and explained the job to him. He was delighted to get the work since, like me, he was between pictures. I arranged for him to be at the Weldon house at ten the next morning and to stay with Buck at all times. Ray was not an overly big man—about six-one and flirting with two hundred pounds. But it was all muscle. He was light on his feet and quick with his hands from a youth spent in the Golden Gloves, and his years as a Vietnam grunt had schooled him in forms of fighting not condoned by the Marquis of Queensbury. If Ray had a flaw it was his temper, which had once gotten him banned from the 20th Century–Fox lot when it had been tested and tweaked by a pretty-boy series lead who had forgotten the tacit rule about being gracious to the cast and crew, and had wound up in Cedars-Sinai hospital taking his meals through a glass straw until his shattered jaw had healed.

I hung up the phone and said to Tori, "Stay with Buck as much as possible. Discourage visitors, but if you can't, at least stay in the room with them."

"Dad and Shelley will love that," she said.

"Whatever you do, don't let him go off on one of his mystery trips. Dope his drink, hide his car keys, call me, but I want him where we can protect him. Damn, it would be a lot easier if we could tell him what's going on."

She just shook her head.

"I know about his pride, Tori. But pride won't mean a damn thing if the cheese really gets binding. How long has he been working on this book?"

"Oh, six or seven weeks. Since his last trip."

I reached out for my copy of *The Avenging Angel*. "He hasn't written anything for a year—since he finished this?" I said, noting the publication date.

"He writes every day. But whenever he finishes a Bart Steele he spends about a year writing something else. I don't know what— he never lets me see it."

"Who does see it? His agent? His publisher?"

"No one. I think maybe he's writing his memoirs."

"Could that have anything to do with what's going on?"

"I've no way of knowing," she said. She stood and came over to me and took the manuscript from my lap, and I could smell her hair when she bent near me. "What are you going to do now?"

"See Sherwin Mandelker, for one thing. And I still have a long list that you gave me." I stood up facing her, very close to her. The top of her head came just below my nose. "You're a peanut, aren't you?" I said.

She moved away. "It's late," she said, "and I have a long drive." She didn't say it with a hell of a lot of conviction, but she did say it.

"I'll walk you to your car."

"That's okay."

"Uh-uh. We have upper-middle-class rapists out here, too. I'll come with you. Unless you'd like to stay and have another drink."

"You know I'd like to," she said, but as I took a step closer she added, "but it is late and I've been told to stay close to my father."

The grace with which I accepted that decision surprised even me as I grabbed my jacket and escorted her out the door. When we were standing curbside at her car and she was fumbling in her purse for her keys I put my hands on her shoulders and when she looked up I kissed her. Very gently, somewhere south of brotherly and north of passionate, but it was good enough for me to call it Our First Kiss, and though she didn't make much of an effort to kiss back, neither did she pull away. When I finally took my lips from her soft mouth she looked up at me and said without rancor, "Damn you, anyway." Then she smiled. It was a halfhearted, begrudging smile but I accepted it gratefully, and then she got into her car and started it up and when she had pulled out of the space and was in the middle of the street she stopped, put the car in neutral, got out again and came back for another, better kiss, and then she was gone again and I stood there in the foggy night with a cold wind just coming up from the nearby sea, and I licked my lips where hers had touched.

The next morning it took half an hour to drive to Mimosa Beach where Deke James's expensive condominium hunkered darkly a block from the ocean. There was an easy, informal quality to the beach cities, and I often went there for recreation—dinner, music, sailing. I wished with all my heart I wasn't down there to talk to Tori Weldon's former husband.

He looked like a wide receiver. He was almost three inches taller than I, and had sun-dappled blond hair that was cut so perfectly it survived showers, ocean swimming and the six miles or so he ran each morning, and still looked like something out of *Gentleman's Quarterly*. Even in midwinter his tan set off his clear blue eyes and straight Pepsodent teeth. His profile was hawklike and his chest and shoulders under the gray hooded sweatshirt he wore were broad and deep, befitting his recent status as a matinee-idol jock. Standing next to him after he'd admitted me to his living room made me feel like a gargoyle on the façade of Notre Dame cathedral.

I declined his offer of a vodka-laced orange juice, and watched while he used his to wash down an alarming number of vitamin pills all at one gulp. We were sitting on his sunporch, which was at this time of year glassed-in with removable picture-window panels. If I craned my neck I probably could have seen the ocean. I didn't bother. I've seen it.

"So," he said, "you're writing about has-beens?"

"That's harsh. I'm just interested in what a guy does when the cheering stops. How he adjusts to being a normal citizen like the rest of us."

"Well, I'm a part-time stockbroker. I was a business major at USC—but I guess you know that."

I didn't, but he was assuming I was the sportswriter I claimed to be, and as such was well-versed on the life and career of one Deke James. "That must seem pretty tame after the NFL," I prompted. If I *had* been doing a story this would be the world's worst interview.

"Oh, I have lots of other interests. I own a few apartment buildings, I have quite an extensive stock portfolio that I work at, I spend lots of time playing with commodities. I still stay in shape, I work out every day, I'm on the Special Olympics Advisory Committee and the President's Committee on Physical Fitness. I'm very active in the SC Alumni Association, and I do some unofficial scouting for both them and the Chargers. I keep busy."

I fawned a little. It was tough. "Looks like there might still be some football left in you."

He nodded sadly. "There is—but since the accident . . ." He stopped. I was obviously supposed to know about that, too. I tried to look sympathetic.

"It was a year and a half ago, right before training camp. There's not much call for a wide receiver with hands like these." He held up his hands, fingers splayed out, palms facing his face, and I almost winced. They were the hands of an elderly arthritic, gnarled, bent and twisted.

"You mind talking about it?"

He waved one of his deformed paws in a vague fashion. "One night on the PCH," he said. I guessed that was beach-town patois for Pacific Coast Highway. "I lost control of the car and rammed into a lightpole. I wasn't even drinking. There was water on the roadway and . . . Anyway, broke my nose, some ribs, lost a tooth—this one," he said, pointing to a capped incisor. "And the hands. They used to say I had the best hands in the league." Bitterness turned down the corners of his patrician mouth, but then he remembered I was the press and he brightened. "The Chargers were really decent about it. As I said, I'm still with the organization as a part-time scout."

I made meaningless notes on my pad. "You live alone?"

He nodded in the affirmative. "I was married for a while, but I didn't like it."

Something stabbed into my gut like icicles, and it took me a moment to realize that Tori had loved this Golden Adonis once, had cared enough to want to spend her lifetime with him, and they had watched sunsets together from this porch, romped on the beach, eaten Sunday breakfasts in bed, walked through the supermarket buying fancy cheeses together and holding hands. He had seen her naked and kissed and touched her in all the places I wanted to. They had probably even screwed on the very sofa I now occupied, and it was all I could do to keep from leaping up. I don't know why the thought had not occurred to me before, but now that it had I was stunned at the amount of pain I was in, and I said tightly, "Can I change my mind about that drink?"

"No prob." He went to fix it while I took deep breaths and tried to get control of my emotions by returning my mind to my case and thinking of Tori as a client. It didn't work. When he brought the drink I gulped down about half of it at once. I've always had a rule about drinking before noon, but these were very special circumstances.

"Wasn't your father-in-law Buck Weldon, the writer?"

Deke nodded, not smiling.

"Do you stay in touch with him?"

"No."

"Why not?"

"Why should I?"

"Did you and he get along?"

"Look," he said pleasantly, "I really don't want to talk about my marriage."

"Neither do I," I said, and had rarely spoken greater truth. "I'm asking about Buck Weldon."

"Especially," he said, "I don't want to talk about Buck Weldon."

"Then you didn't get along?"

"Not much."

"Why?"

"Off the record, he is one mean son of a bitch."

"In what way?"

"In every way—now what else did you want to talk about?" There was tightness in his voice, as though he were under as much of an emotional strain right then as I was.

"I know no one likes their in-laws, Deke, but was there some special—?"

"Look, let's drop it!"

"Sure. But this is human-interest stuff. Two famous celebrities in the same family. The readers will eat it up."

"The readers can eat shit! Change the subject."

"My reporter's instincts tell me I'm on to something here, Deke."

"Your reporter's instincts are going to get your ass tossed out of here in a minute. I don't want to talk about my marriage or Buck Weldon or his cunt daughter."

I tried not to take umbrage at that. Tried hard. I wasn't successful. I pressed on. "Not very gentlemanly of you to say, Deke. What would your loyal fans think?"

He stood up, the affability that had remained dropping from him like a discarded cloak. "That's it," he said.

"Take it easy."

"This interview's over. This stuff is no one's business."

"I've always found the stuff that's no one's business is the most interesting, Deke. Like the beef between you and Weldon."

"Hit the bricks, pal."

"I seem to have picked open a scab."

He wrested the drink from my hand, and some of it spilled on my fingers. It was sticky and unpleasant. "Out!"

"What're you getting so—?"

"Get the fuck out of my house," he said, "before I get nasty."

"Too late," I said.

I stood and went toward the door very casually, as if it were my own idea. He was behind me, step for step. "Who sent you?" he demanded. "You're not from Hearst." I ignored him. I stepped up on the riser by his front door but before I could get my hand on the knob he'd grabbed me by the left bicep and spun me around. Standing up on the riser I was a shade taller than he.

"I'm not accustomed to asking questions and having them ignored," he said.

"There's always a first time."

"Answer me, you bastard!" He increased the pressure on my arm. I dislike being touched by anyone that I don't want to touch me. I looked pointedly down at his hand on my arm but he didn't take the hint. "Did Buck Weldon send you here?" he demanded. "Or was it the Ice Princess?"

His fingers digging into my muscle started to hurt. I was glad. I'm a guy who needs lots of motivation. I hit him one short punch, in the ribs right under the heart. I wondered whether those were the two ribs that had been broken. It took him completely unawares and he stumbled backward, not losing his footing but looking very awkward in the process, probably another first for Deke James. He leaned against the back of a chair, pressing the spot where I'd hit him, and I reflected on one of the many differences between baseball and football. A baseball player never rubs where it hurts. It's a matter of professional pride.

I didn't leave right away, I just stood there as he stared dully at me from under darkening brows; it was only fair that I give him the opportunity to do something about it if he wanted to. He didn't. I was grateful that if Tori had to have married a professional football player he had been a wide receiver. An offensive lineman would've torn off my face. I flexed my right fist, the one I'd hit him with. I guess I have pretty good hands myself.

"You'll hear from my lawyer," he said. He was obviously in pain. I waved and let myself out.

I walked the block down to the Esplanade and shared a bench with an old man wrapped in a sweater and muffler, and smoked my first cigarette of the day, looking across the beach to the broad expanse of ocean, dark gray against a light sky. The waves were about four feet high, and even in mid-December there were a scattered few die-hard surfers in black rubber wet suits trying to catch one of those waves, but the Pacific paid them no heed as it went about its business, whitecaps turning dark as the current churned up loose bottom sand. The sound and smell revitalized me. By nature I am nonviolent, and I take little pride in hitting people, even ex-husbands. But I wasn't ashamed of how good I felt at having hit Deke James.

I passed the time of day with my benchmate for a bit. He was a retired chiropractor, he told me, and had fulfilled a lifelong dream of living at the ocean when he'd retired six years ago. I told him I loved the beach, too, which wasn't entirely true. I love to be near the water, but I hate suntan oil and wet sand and overmuscled teenagers who hit you with their Frisbee because they just don't care and mothers who take down their four-year-olds' pants to put on their bathing suits in full view of ten thousand people. I wished the doc a happy retirement and walked down to a quaint little shopping center with two French pâtisseries and a fancy pizza-to-go place and I had a croissant and coffee to wash away the taste of the vodka-laced orange juice, and then I called Jo at the office.

"How's Marsh?"

"He's great. Back to work today. He bounces back—it's amazing. Behind that wimpy exterior is a pretty tough little guy."

"That's good," I said. "Jo, I want you to call the LA *Times* and find out the date of Deke James's automobile accident—should be a year ago last June or so. Then call the highway patrol and get hold of the accident report. It was in Mimosa Beach on the PCH."

"The what?"

I explained. Chameleonlike, I tend to take on the habits and customs of wherever I happen to be at the moment. I was probably just a step away from baggie surfing trunks and zoris. "Find out what hospital he was taken to and see if you can get the medical report."

I heard her breathing as she wrote. Then she asked who Deke James was and I told her. "Then," I finished up, "call around to some industry people—maybe someone at *Variety*—and find out where Sherwin Mandelker hangs out."

"He's got offices at Mercury."

"I know, but he won't see me there. I have to take him by surprise—socially. And get me a phone number on Jeffrey Quinn."

"The actor? What's he got to do with Buck Weldon?"

"Jo, I'll be in the office later today and tell you all about it."

"You and your secrets."

"Being mysterious makes me sexier."

"I hadn't noticed."

The address Tori had given me for her sister was a small apartment building on Ohio Avenue about a mile from the Westwood Village shopping area and the UCLA campus. Getting there from Mimosa Beach almost required a passport, but it took me less than an hour and I had some time to kill before my appointment with Professor Kullander.

Valerie Weldon was blond, like Tori, but there the resemblance ended. Her eyes were big and blue, her mouth was too hard for the rest of her baby face, and though still in her late teens she had the lush, swelling breasts and hips that Bart Steele might fall for. She was well aware of the effect she had on males, her unfettered breasts jutting against the man's shirt she wore hanging outside her designer jeans. She allowed as how Tori had mentioned I would be getting in touch with her.

"But she didn't tell me what a fox you are," Valerie added.

For a brief flicker I was flattered by the obvious interest she was showing in me, but then it turned me off. I was almost certain that with Valerie Weldon flirtation was automatic. It was nothing I could take personally. Or wanted to.

I looked around the apartment. There was a large sketchpad on an easel, and several charcoal sketches tossed around the room carelessly. They were all of the same subject—a lithe young black man. In one of the sketches he wore a posing strap. In the others he didn't.

"These are pretty good, Valerie," I said. "Your sister mentioned you were an artist."

"That's because she's ashamed to tell people what I really am," Valerie said.

"What's that?"

"A bum." She sat down on the rattan sofa and indicated I should sit next to her. "I hear someone's gunning for the old man," she said.

"That's pretty cold, isn't it?"

"Why pussyfoot around? It saves time. What can I tell you about it?"

"I don't know. What can you?"

"Not much. Except that he's got bucks and he's a celebrity, and that makes enemies."

"Anyone in particular?"

"Could be a hundred people. I don't know, I'm not around there much."

"How come?"

"I don't want to hang out with my *dad*," she said, appalled. "I'm a big girl now. Or didn't you notice?" A bit arch, but she made her point.

"Val, lots of people have enemies, but murder is another story. Anyone you can think of that really hates your father?"

She shrugged and lit a cigarette, holding it like a joint, and leaned back against the backrest of the sofa to emphasize her best points. "He screws around a lot. Some chick didn't like it, maybe. Or some chick's husband."

"That's not much help."

"Look, if I knew who was trying to kill my father I'd tell you, wouldn't I?"

"What about Deke James?"

"Tori's Deke James? He's a prick, but I don't think he's killer material."

"Why is he a prick? In what way?"

"Ask Tori. I wasn't married to him."

"He doesn't like Buck very much, does he?"

She chuckled. "You can sing that in G."

"Why not?"

She stood up and walked over to the window for no particular reason. Evasive action if I'd ever seen it. "The divorce wasn't nice. Dad was on Tori's side. So Deke doesn't like him. No biggie."

"Do you like him, Valerie?"

"Val. Everybody calls me Val. Sure I like him. He's my father. He's a pretty good old bird—as old birds go." She batted her baby blues at me and sat down again, reaching over as she did to brush back a stray lock of hair that had fallen on my forehead. Her timing was terrific. I heard a key in the door and looked up to see a young black man coming in. He wore a dashiki that flowed over the musculature of his body, and his hair was in a modified Afro. I recognized him at once from Valerie's sketches. He stopped in the doorway and stared at me through his dark glasses. Val had managed to get her hand away from my face before he'd come all the way in, but we somehow *looked* like we'd been doing something wrong, as though an echo of her gesture with my hair still hung in the room.

Val jumped to her feet, more flustered than was absolutely necessary. "This is my friend Abdul Muhammad," she said. "Abdul, this is Mr. Saxon. He's a friend of my sister."

I stood up for a handshake but Abdul ignored both me and my hand. "What's he want?" he said. His voice was a rumbly Barry White basso.

"Just some family problems."

"Why he coming around here?"

I dislike being talked about as if I weren't in the room. "A friend of the family," I said.

"Shit!" Abdul said. "He look like the Man."

"Something like that," I said. I produced one of my business cards but he neither took it nor looked at it. "Do you know Val's father?"

"He don't want to know me," Abdul said, addressing me directly for the first time. "And I don't wanna know him either. Or you." To Val he said, "I'll be back later."

He started out the door and Val said, "Wait," and the two of them went out into the hall and I could hear them talking in low tones outside the door, Abdul's voice angry and hers placating. I contemplated sitting back down but decided I was happier on my feet, so I stood there until they finished outside and Val came back in alone. She shrugged, disclaiming any responsibility for Abdul's bad manners.

"What a personality that guy needs!" I said.

"Abdul's a professional student," she said, as if it explained everything, "and an amateur revolutionary. Half the time I don't know what he's talking about. He gets jealous sometimes. He'll be okay."

"I can't tell you how relieved I am to hear it."

She came up very close to me, the tips of her breasts touching my chest. "You're pretty funny," she said.

"Wait till you hear me do my fag-at-the-prizefight routine."

"Foxy, too. Maybe we could give Abdul something to be jealous about sometime?"

"There are about twenty-five reasons why that isn't going to happen, Val," I told her, "and twenty of them are years."

"That's bullshit."

"Nevertheless," I said. I still had my card in my hand and I gave it to her. "I'm trying to keep your father alive and that means I need to know all the people who might want it otherwise. If you hear anything or think of anything, call me—day or night."

"I prefer night, I think." She was like me in one way. She never gave up.

"You're taking this rather lightly, aren't you?" I said. "Considering someone's trying to snuff your father."

She finally moved away a bit, the deliberate brutality of my remark having an almost physical effect on her. "Dad and I have an agreement," she said. "He stays out of my business and I stay out of his. We don't ask questions we don't want to hear the answers to."

"Wouldn't you like the answer to who's trying to kill him?"

"Sure. But there's nothing I can do about it one way or the other. So it's best I don't get all bummed."

Bummed. God, I love California! "What about Abdul? Would he want to hurt your father for any reason?"

"Dad is white and rich. That makes him automatically shit in Abdul's book. But Dad supports me and I support Abdul, and he isn't so radical that he's going to want to kill off his meal ticket."

"*Why* do you support Abdul? He looks big enough to take care of himself."

"Because he's lots more fun than a puppy or a kitten, and I've almost got him trained not to mess on the floor." Her look was defiant, yet playful. I really didn't like her very much. I reached out and touched her left breast with the end of my forefinger, then quickly removed it.

"Not that I'm offended," she said, "but what was that for?"

"I just wanted to see if you were cold to the touch," I said.

Out on the street I lit another cigarette. I was only smoking them when I really needed them. I looked at my watch. It was almost time for me to meet with Bo Kullander and I wanted to leave myself a little extra time because I often get lost strolling around the enormous UCLA campus.

But Abdul Muhammad had different ideas. He came up to me

almost as soon as I was out the door, moving like an athlete, with a glower that was meant to be intimidating.

"Hey!" he said, and it came out like the crack of a drover's whip. "Hey, man!"

"Hello there, Abdul," I said. Yes, it was condescending. It was meant to be. A simple and innocuous "hello" is always turned into a putdown by the simple addendum of the word *there*. It goes hand in hand with patting a child on the head. I suppose I shouldn't have said it, but Abdul hadn't exactly been Mr. Congeniality up in Val's apartment, and I was in no mood to make nice with him now.

"Stay away from my squeeze, man," he said, "or you and me is going to tangle."

"I think you've got the wrong idea—"

"You just keep it in mind. Hear me?"

"Of course I hear you, Abdul. You're shouting."

"Don' fuck with me, man, I ain't joking!"

"You could have fooled me, Abdul," I said. I don't know why I used his name in every sentence. When someone has an ordinary name like Bob or Jim or Michael people pretty much ignore it. But talk to anyone with an unusual name like Bonar or Leverett or Abdul and you find yourself saying it a lot. I remember once in a bar in Ladera Beach when a woman walked in and almost everyone in the place said "Hi, January," or "Hello, January," or, "Hey, January, there's a seat over here!" I sat in that bar for three hours and heard no choruses of "Hi, Debbie" or "Hi, Tom." But everyone *wanted* to say January, and I suppose I wanted to say Abdul. What I really wanted was to get the hell out of there.

"I'll hurt you, man," he was saying. His arms hung loosely at his sides and slightly away from his body like an old-fashioned frontier gunfighter's, and suddenly he didn't look revolutionary and dangerous, he only looked foolish and young and angry, and I realized he was no streetwise ghetto punk with a cause but a middle-class black college student who spoke perfect English and probably maintained a B average, who depended on his stud good looks and the mystique of a Cause to keep him supplied with sex, drugs and a place to hang out at the expense of Valerie Weldon, and who was banking on the gut-level fear most whites have of big, muscular black men to scare me away from his meal ticket. I tried to re-member the last time I'd punched two different people in the course of a single morning, but the memory eluded me. I finally decided if I wanted to take Abdul, I could. I just didn't want to.

"Not now, Abdul, I've got a headache."

I brushed past him and walked down the sidewalk toward my car. I didn't bother looking around to see whether or not he was coming after me. I somehow knew he was not. When I unlocked my door and slid under the steering wheel I could see him through the windshield, just about where I'd left him, still in that same, silly "Go for your gun, Marshal" pose. As I started the car I couldn't help but reflect that of the four people I had interviewed regarding the Buck Weldon matter, two of them had wanted to hurt me and two had wanted to fuck me. I nurtured a fond hope that Professor Kullander was not going to fall into either of the existing catego-ries.

I hadn't really been expecting to meet a stuffy, absentminded academician or a tweedy, pipe-sucking pedant, but Bo Kullander was a breath of fresh air anyway. He was extremely tall and hearty, with graying blond hair and blue eyes that crinkled at the corners and seemed always to be secretly amused. He was wearing a bright blue Dodger jacket over a T-shirt that sang the praises of the UCLA Bruins. He ushered me into his office, a cubbyhole in the English Department, and we shared coffee from his thermos while he ate a healthy-looking sandwich made up of all sorts of vegetable matter on dark, thick brown bread.

I showed him my license and told him I was doing some work that involved Buck Weldon and needed some information of a lit-erary nature, and that I was grateful he understood the need for confidentiality and didn't press me for the details of my investiga-tion nor the identity of my client. "In what way may I be of help, Mr. Saxon?" he said. The Swedish accent was almost all gone, but there was still the slight aftertaste of *grävlax,* just enough to make people really listen when he spoke. He had what can best be de-scribed as a rather merry baritone voice.

"I'm trying to get a handle on Weldon's work—is there a central theme that runs through his writings, some single note that makes a Buck Weldon mystery different from, say, a Ross McDonald?"

Kullander pushed a few errant strands of alfalfa sprouts into the corner of his mouth and chewed for a while, thinking. He finally volunteered, "I think Weldon is one of the most American of American writers, if you know what I mean?"

"Like Steinbeck?"

"Not exactly. Steinbeck wrote about America and he wrote about grassroots Americans, but he did so with the sensibility of a European—politically sophisticated, liberally motivated, interested in the great social themes of his time and anxious to make a difference. But Buck Weldon writes as a pure Yankee. His themes are rugged individualism, vigilante law, and the moral code of a hero who is not always particularly likable but always, in his author's perspective, on the side of the angels. His women are either idealized sex objects or pure villainesses. He deals with revenge, justice, the righting of wrongs no matter what the personal cost. And, excepting the Knights of the Table Round, that is a uniquely American outlook. That is why, being a European, I am so fascinated with his work. America, as I'm sure you know, has always been more eager to espouse right-wing ideals than those of the left, as opposed to the more liberal traditions of the Continent; what we have in Bart Steele is the pure, distilled essence of those ideals—the Fascist as role model. And just as you suspend logic and principle and reason and history to cheer for the Confederacy as you read *Gone With the Wind,* no matter what your personal political convictions, so you perceive Bart Steele, who maims and kills and fornicates indiscriminately to achieve his own ends, as on the side of right and order. His ends always justify his means, no matter how unpalatable those means might appear in a nonfictional context."

"Whew!" I said.

"As a teacher and student and critic of literature my job is rather like that of Bart Steele—or like yours—a kind of literary detective, putting all the clues together and trying to come up with the truth. It's fun, especially with Buck Weldon. Whatever else his writing may be, it's damned fine escape entertainment."

"I'm told you know Buck Weldon personally?"

"We've sat and argued many a night, yes. I usually lose—I can't hold my liquor the way he can."

"How did you meet him?"

Kullander finished his sandwich and mopped the mayonnaise off his mouth with a wadded-up paper napkin, then put it into the bag in which his sandwich had come and threw the whole business into the wastebasket. "Several years ago I became interested in the whole so-called 'private eye' genre, and instantly became enamored of Bart Steele for all the reasons I've just outlined. I was preparing a paper on the subject and called Mr. Weldon to let him read it before I presented it. He was flattered to be considered worthy of attention from a prestigious university like this one. He said most people read his work either on an airplane or on the toilet. Anyway, we became close. In many ways we think identically, especially when it comes to writing. Siamese twins joined at the mind, as it were."

"You find Buck to be as right-wing as his books?"

"Not entirely. But he certainly believes in the concept of virtue triumphant and he deplores the liberal drift this country was taking during the sixties and seventies."

"His writing reflects that?"

"Yes of course it does," Kullander said. "But there's more to it than that. Look past the sex and sadism that has made Buck Weldon a shockingly rich man and you will, on occasion, find that he writes with a scalpel, so sharp that the words can cause real pain." He refilled our coffee cups from the thermos.

"You like him very much, don't you?"

"The man is a delight. He never fails to stimulate."

"Do you think, Professor, that Weldon would ever use Bart Steele's methods to see that the Right Thing was done?"

He frowned. "I believe he's ready to fight for what he believes. Is that what you mean?"

"To your knowledge, has he ever done anything or written anything that might provoke retaliation or revenge?"

"Like Mailer and Hemingway, he's had his barroom fisticuffs— but I don't think anyone holds a grudge about those."

"Anything in his work, past or present, that would provoke anyone to want to hurt him personally?"

He laughed, a deep chuckle. "My God, the man writes detective novels. He's not Eldridge Cleaver or Germaine Greer. He may be right-wing but I hardly think he's inflammatory. Bart Steele books will not change the world like Steinbeck's *Grapes of Wrath* or Sinclair's *The Jungle* or Jack Kale's *Silver Mountain*."

I felt I was getting nowhere in terms of the case, although it was exciting for me to talk literature with one as knowledgeable as Bo Kullander. I ruefully got the conversation away from Buck's work and back to Buck personally.

"Is there anyone you know who dislikes Buck a lot?"

"Personally, you mean?"

"Personally."

Kullander frowned. "This sounds serious."

"It could be, Professor."

"Well, I don't see Buck that much to know who his friends and enemies are. I know his ex-son-in-law has no love for him."

"Deke James?"

"When he and Buck's daughter first married Buck was proud as a peacock that he had a genuine star in his family. It almost made up for his having sired only girls. And Deke James was a charming fellow socially. Apparently, though, he had a terrible temper. It was my understanding after the divorce that whenever James dropped a pass in the end zone on a Sunday, poor Tori was in for a belting-around. Buck hates James for that, of course, and let him know it." And I hated Deke James for it even more.

"Tori," Kullander said, "is, I think, the only person Buck truly cares about."

I found myself wishing I'd hit Deke a lot harder that morning.

When I returned to my office Jo was waiting for me with a stack of messages and several pages of notes that she refused to give me until I'd told her everything that was going on. There were dark smudges of exhaustion under her brown eyes, but she seemed to have survived Marsh's close call the way she got through everything else—like a champ.

She trotted after me to my desk, anxious to give me all her news.

"First," she said, handing me a pink message slip, "here's Jeffrey Quinn's phone number, and he is in town. Secondly, Mr. Sherwin

Mandelker has dinner almost every night he's in Los Angeles at the Beverly Canyon Room, where he is treated like the absolute monarch that he is. You could probably talk to him there."

"Great," I said. "Would you make a reservation for eight o'clock tonight. For two."

Her eyebrows went up and she smiled. "Two? Hmmm. I guess finally you're getting over whatsername and are ready to sit up and take nourishment." Jo had never liked Leila. She handed me another message slip. "Lieutenant DiMattia would like to talk to you at your earliest convenience."

"Is that what he said?"

"No, he said to tell you to get your ass on the phone."

"That's more like it," I said.

"Now, as to this Deke James . . ." She consulted her legal pad, which was covered with her handwriting. "Deke James was admitted to Saint John's emergency room at nine-fifty P.M. on June twenty-second of last year, and was treated for a broken nose, two fractured ribs, ten badly broken fingers and a sprained wrist, plus multiple contusions of the face and abdomen and a broken tooth. He spent the night under observation and was released the following morning. One week later he held a press conference in San Diego to announce that, due to his injuries, he was retiring from football as an active player." She smiled her innocent, wicked smile. "From the newspaper accounts there wasn't a dry eye in the house." And then she stood there looking smug as hell, the canary feathers plastered all over her face, and I knew she had a kicker. Jo always had a kicker.

"Out with it, woman!" I said.

"I contacted the local beach police departments and the Chippies. No one seems to have any record of a vehicular accident on June twenty-second or any date near it that involved Deke James."

"Are you telling me Deke James never had an automobile accident?"

"No, sir," she said in her best secretaryese. "I'm telling you he didn't have one a year ago June on the Pacific Coast Highway."

I leaned back in my chair and beamed at my assistant with whom I was well pleased. "Jo," I said, "you're the eighth wonder of the world."

"That must be why you pay me so much," she said, and went back out to her own desk to make my dinner reservations. I called Tori on the other line and asked her to meet me in town that evening.

"For a very elegant dinner," I said, "and hopefully some information. And look especially terrific—not just merely spectacular like you usually do."

"Does this have anything to do with my father?" she said. "Or are you trying to manipulate me into having dinner with you again?"

"The very suggestion is beneath contempt," I told her. "I can't wait to see you again—but this *is* business."

Then I called Joe DiMattia at LAPD.

"Two things, cockbreath," he said brusquely. It was always so nice to talk to Lieutenant DiMattia. "Douglas at West Valley says there were no other reports of random shootings in the Valley the night of the Weldon incident. That kind of blows your theory about joyriding teenagers."

"It was never my theory, Joe. It was just mentioned as a possibility."

"Jesus, Saxon, you make my balls ache. The other thing is, there's muscle hanging around Weldon's house all day today. A tan Firebird registered to—"

"Raymond Tucek. It's okay, Joe, he's mine, private security."

"You might have let us know, dipshit!"

"Why? Did you roust him?"

"No—no reason to."

"Good—he'll be back tomorrow, probably in a different car. Now that you know the other night was a planned hit, what are you going to do about it?"

"There's nothing we can do. Besides, your gorilla is looking out for things." His voice got softer and reedier. "Saxon, are you keeping any secrets from me?"

"My life is an open book, Lieutenant. As a matter of fact . . ." I couldn't resist the needle. "There are some passages that you, especially, might find rather enlightening."

He terminated the call with the same instructions on what I could do to myself that he'd given me the last time. I was frankly disappointed. Since he'd begun the conversation with "cockbreath" and peaked it with "dipshit," I'd been expecting a sign-off a little more creative.

When I got back to my apartment I checked my answering machine—no calls—and then called Jeff Quinn. We had never been close friends but we'd seen each other around and he knew who I was. He sounded genuinely glad to hear from me.

"The phone doesn't ring that often any more," he said.

"I know, Jeff, I'm sure it's been rough. That's the price you pay for guts."

"All guts and no brains, I guess." Fortunately Jeff had lots of money of his own and had married into a great deal more, so no one was running a tag day for him. But actors, present company included, are ninety-five percent ego, and not working for so long must have ground him pretty hard. "What's up?"

"Jeff, between gigs I run a little detective agency on the side."

"I think I heard that someplace, yeah."

"Well, I'm on a case and your name came up."

He snorted. "First time my name's come up in this town for a long time."

I told him about Buck Weldon's book. He didn't say anything for a while. Then he said, "Am I a black hat or a white hat?"

"Well, Bart Steele's the hero, but as far as I can tell, you're one of the good guys."

"Whew," he said, not without sarcasm.

"Jeff, you didn't know about this, did you?"

"I don't know about anything any more. I'm not exactly au courant in the business, you know. When you're an outie in this down, your friends disappear into the mist like Brigadoon. Jesus, life is funny. About eight years ago they talked to my agent about me playing Bart Steele on a TV series. I was hot then, doing features, and I didn't want to get tied down on a TV show—then the series never got made anyway. And now here I am—*in* a Bart Steele book."

I showered and poured myself a drink and then I sat around in my Japanese *fukota* and thought about Jeff and how unfair life was, and how lousy an industry was that used people up and then threw them away like snotty Kleenex.

I dressed slowly, in my only suit, a charcoal-gray one I'd had made for me in Hong Kong a few years earlier. In Los Angeles it is rare that one has to wear a suit unless one is in investment banking or the mortuary business, and it had been at least eight months since I'd put on this one. I was dismayed that it was a bit more snug around the waist than I remembered, and I made a mental note to cut down on my drinking and eating. However, with the jacket on it looked sharp, befitting a man on his way to dine with an incredibly beautiful woman at the incredibly expensive Beverly Canyon Room to talk to the incredibly important Sherwin Mandelker. I ran a brush through my hair and headed out.

I met Tori in the cocktail lounge of a hotel at the juncture of Sunset and the freeway. It was a good halfway point, and although I felt vaguely guilty about not picking her up at her place, she'd assured me it would be best if her father didn't see me and that it was a sixty-mile round trip from the Palisades to Verdant Hills. I was dizzied at the sight of her in a peach-colored pantsuit with batwing sleeves that made her look extraterrestrial. We had some time before our dinner reservation and so we had a drink at the hotel.

"Just what is it we're supposed to accomplish tonight?" she asked.

"We're going to talk to Mr. Mandelker. Or rather I am. That's all."

"About what?"

"Life. Movies. Books. Embezzlement. I don't know, we'll play it by ear."

"Valerie said you were by to see her today."

"Valerie said the truth."

"She said her boyfriend got all bent out of shape about you. She also said you were adorable."

It was getting worse. Now I was no longer merely cute.

"Is it much of an effort for you to charm every woman you see?"

"It comes naturally," I said, and then I got angry. "Damn it, you've got no call to say that to me. I wasn't trying to put the make on your sister."

"You could have, you know. She was impressed."

"I have a pair of socks at home older than her. Besides, right now you are the only woman that impresses me."

"Sure," she said.

"Yes, sure! Why are you so positive that I'm insincere?"

"I'm not—I've just heard it all before and I get tired of it. Look, you promised this was going to be strictly business. I don't want to sit here and hassle with you about getting into a relationship or not getting into—"

"Okay, I'll stop," I said. "But you'd better be very careful about me, Tori."

"Why?"

"Because," I said, "I might make you happy."

The Beverly Canyon Room was on Cañon Drive, a street in the heart of Beverly Hills whose name was invariably mispronounced "Cannon" Drive by the locals, ignoring the squiggle over the n, in the same fashion they pronounced the name of Cabrillo Beach as though it were something with which to scour a roasting pan. The restaurant itself hid behind a façade so plain it was almost secretive, its only identification a small bronze plaque near the door, presumably to discourage tourists and those who were not in the Hollywood inner circle. Inside, a supercilious maitre d' presided over his station in an atrium stocked with enough large-leafed plants to decorate the set of a Tarzan movie. I had been there once before, and I knew for a fact there was always, at all times, a fresh load of bar ice in the urinals of the men's room, the sure sign of a very classy restaurant.

We were seated at a not-too-good table by a captain whose attitude let us know we were lucky to be getting in at all. What probably saved us from a seat behind the kitchen door was that, in a town of beautiful women, Tori Weldon was a standout, and her fresh and unusual looks stood as a marked contrast to the Beverly Hills matrons who spent most of their days being pummeled by

Birgitta, coiffed by Jean-Paul, made up by José and clad by Enrico. I was damned proud to be seen with her.

My interest, however, was focused on the large corner booth, the one that gave its occupants a clear view of everything else in the room. It was vacant at the moment, but I knew its RESERVED table card was there for Sherwin Mandelker.

"You don't expect Mandelker to admit he's trying to kill my father, do you?" Tori said when we were finally seated.

"Naturally not. I'm not even sure that he is. But I've played some penny-ante poker in my day, and I know that when you get people nervous they get careless and sometimes tip their hands."

"And you say that ploys are beneath you!"

"When it comes to you they are," I said. "I'm being as honest as I can. I just wish we'd met at a party or in church or in an elevator or in some cheap bar instead of the way we did. But it doesn't matter, because I really like being with you."

"I wish you didn't."

"Why?"

"Because I like being with you, too, and it would complicate things a lot less if you didn't feel the same way."

"Why is that a complication?"

"I've spent a lot of my life avoiding getting hurt," she explained. "When you keep the doors and windows locked you can keep out the wind and rain."

"True," I said, "but then you never know when the sun comes out."

"At least you avoid getting sunburned," she said, and there was sadness in her eyes.

I felt the conversation getting heavier than I wanted it to. To lighten it up I said, "How about if I spring for a jar of Noxzema?" and it made her laugh in spite of herself.

There was a stirring at the front door and Sherwin Mandelker and his party came in. I put my hand on Tori's arm and nodded toward them as they made their way through the Canyon Room, Mandelker in the lead, followed by a vapidly attractive young woman who bore the unmistakable stamp of Hollywood starlet like a mark of Cain on her forehead. Behind her was a well-tanned and immaculately barbered man of about fifty whom I immediately hated because his gray hair was prettier than mine, and a woman who was obviously his wife because she was too old and unattractive to be his girlfriend. But it was Mandelker who interested me the most. Suited in a dark gray pinstripe that must have cost eight hundred dollars and was cut to minimize his portly shortness, he kept his eyes practically hidden behind wire-rimmed spectacles. His cheeks glowed with a recent facial and his hair looked as though it were trimmed every few days. Like so many other men in this room he radiated affluence and power, but even in their company Sherwin Mandelker was his own kind of superstar.

I couldn't help noticing the party that came in immediately after the Mandelker group, two large, muscular men wearing cheap dark suits, escorting two hard-looking women. It was hard to imagine the Canyon Room even letting them in, but they were placed at a table in the middle of the room on a direct sight line with Mandelker's booth. The penetrating glances they sent around the room, scrutinizing everyone in the place, were not those of tourists rubbernecking movie stars. They were obviously on Mandelker's payroll—the price he had to pay for being an outrageous crook who got away with it.

After Mandelker had seated himself, he allowed those people in the room whom he knew a small wave or a nod. No one had to tell him that, among the big brass, he was solid gold. He wore his celebrity and his notoriety like an ermine cloak. He glanced at me for a split second, probably trying to place me, and since he couldn't right away I was obviously unimportant enough to be dismissed. His eyes lingered on Tori a bit longer, admiring and inquiring, but since he couldn't place her either and since she was definitely not of the starlet stamp he dismissed her, too. The captain hovered at his table much longer than he had when he'd seated us, and within seconds two waiters and the wine steward were also in attendance. It was the kind of VIP treatment one saw only in Beverly Hills. It frankly repelled me, and I hoped with all my heart that if things ever changed for me in my acting career, if I really got lucky and hit the heights of superstardom, I would eschew the kind of treatment I saw Mandelker getting. It was probably a vain hope. I've always found that when people persist in kissing your ass, you gradually come around to the belief that it is only your due.

It annoyed the hell out of me that Mandelker's order was taken before ours, even though we had preceded him into the restaurant by at least ten minutes, something I might have made a fuss about under different circumstances. But when the minyan of restaurant employees had finally departed from the Mandelker booth, the parade began in earnest. Half the people in the Beverly Canyon Room found their way to the corner booth to pay homage and swear fealty and beg royal favor or patronage as a group of merchant princes might have of a Renaissance pope. Most of them Mandelker received with a kind of distant grace, not even bothering to shake hands, accepting their well wishes as befitted his rank. I studied the faces of the men and women who approached him, many of whom I knew by sight, and their eyes and the up- or downturn of their mouths as they returned to their own dinner companions usually indicated whether they felt the encounter with Mandelker had been successful or not in terms of their own careers and ambitions and greeds. They were indeed a self-serving lot, and their awe of Sherwin Mandelker, even in the light of their own high positions of power and wealth, was simply amazing to me. If there was royalty in the industry, Mandelker was the *capo di tutti capi* among the deal-makers and career-breakers. The fact that he had openly and joyfully committed embezzlement and had come out of it not only unscathed but better off than before only served to stoke the fires of his legend.

Mandelker's two employees scrutinized every visitor to his table. If it were an established performer or a well-known studio or network executive, they remained calm and relaxed, or as much so as they could get. If they were not familiar with the person who approached their boss they would sit almost imperceptibly straighter and at such an angle to their table that they could get to their feet and across the room within seconds.

Our food finally came, filet of sole for Tori and blanquette of veal for me. Both were competently if indifferently prepared, but that was no surprise. After all, people did not patronize the Beverly Canyon Room for the haute cuisine, but to congratulate themselves that they were successful enough to afford to be there, to nod and wave and press flesh in a year-round Easter Parade.

"Are you going to talk to him or are we just looking?" Tori said.

"Let me digest my dinner first. Don't worry, he'll be here for a while. They've just brought the coffees. How about some dessert?"

"Dessert?" she said. "You know, we keep seeing each other in restaurants. I'm afraid if I hang around with you much longer I'm going to eat myself into a sideshow."

"Not to worry," I said, covering her hand with mine. "You're the most fabulous-looking woman in the place. In Beverly Hills. In the state of California, even."

"Tomorrow the world."

"Nope, sorry. There is one woman in the world even lovelier than you. Unfortunately for me, she lives in Finland and has a thing for big, hunky, hairy reindeer wranglers."

They brought our coffee and two chocolate mints wrapped in green foil. I ate them both. I was on my second cup of coffee when I noticed a lull in the sycophantic procession to Mandelker's table and decided to fill it. I stood up, buttoned my jacket, gave Tori's hand a squeeze and made my way through the tables to Mandelker and his friends. When I slowed down I saw out of the corner of my eye an immediate alertness on the part of the two bodyguards. They didn't know me and were unsure as to whether I was worthy of breathing the same air as their boss. Though neither made a move to rise, I felt their mean, hard eyes on me.

"Good evening, Mr. Mandelker," I said. He glanced up and a slight frown made a little neat crease between his eyebrows. I nodded a perfunctory hello to the others at the table.

"I've seen you in something, I know, but the name escapes me," Mandelker said. He spoke so softly that I had to lean forward to hear him. The light flashed on the flat lenses of his glasses.

"Saxon," I told him.

"Oh, yeah, how are you?" And then he looked away in a way that unmistakably spelled dismissal. A second later he looked back up at me, surprised I was still there, and not pleased.

"I'm a friend of Buck Weldon's."

"Well, good for you."

The condescending bastard! "You know who he is?"

The voice was still soft but there was a core of steel in it. "I didn't just fall off the turnip truck. Of course I know who he is."

"Do you also know that he's writing a book about you?"

"Oh, Christ, another one?"

I waited. Then I said, "How do you feel about that?"

"Flattered and humble, okay? If you'll excuse us—"

"You wouldn't be flattered if you read it."

"I have no intention of reading it. Look, what do you want here, Saxon?"

"Nothing."

His eyes moved quickly to the bodyguards across the room, but he made no overt gesture to them. "Is this some kind of cheap shakedown? I don't like shakedowns."

I don't mind admitting that the man's arrogance, his haughty certainty that he was one of the chosen, pricked me in a way I didn't like for one minute. It was hard to remain cool and unemotional as one in my profession is supposed to do. "I don't recall asking you for anything."

"Yeah, well," he said, and waved me away, "it's early yet."

"I'm just telling you as a friend."

"I don't have day players for friends," he said.

"Your loss."

"Look," he said, getting annoyed, "I'm touched by your concern, but we're trying to eat our dinner here—so fuck off."

The wife of the silver-haired man jumped, and her husband looked discomfited. I had a feeling he was a Big Board type Mandelker was wooing as a prospective financial backer for a film project, the proverbial butter-and-egg man, and that down on Spring Street at the exchange they didn't tell each other to fuck off, at least not in so many words. I tried to accept my abrupt dismissal with more dignity than he had offered it with. It was tough.

Tori's eyes were green saucers when I returned to her. Our table was too far from Mandelker's for her to have overheard what was said, but she had caught the tenor of the encounter through our body language. "I think you made him mad," she said.

"We don't exactly have a tennis date." I looked back at Mandelker, who was talking to the silver-haired man. The starlet was inhaling her cheesecake and the older lady was staring at me as though I'd flashed her on the subway. The bodyguards were giving me that look usually reserved for mealy bugs in the escarole, and the restaurant's staff kept their eyes averted the way one does from

an eccentric uncle who's just told the vicar at tea about his consti-
pation problems and his last really satisfying dump in 1953. I decided I'd overstayed my welcome at the posh Beverly Canyon
Room, and I signaled for the check.

There was no way out of the restaurant except past Mandelker's
booth, and I couldn't resist a final needle. "One thing should please
you, Mr. Mandelker," I said. "You're much better looking in the
book." The flush under Mandelker's artificially tanned cheeks
pleased me, I know that. My propensity for wise-asshood had led
me into a certain amount of trouble over the years, physical as well
as financial. There was an imp of the perverse deep within me that
made me say things like that.

It took a few minutes for the parking attendant to find my car,
probably because he'd parked it somewhere far away where it
wouldn't contaminate the Bentleys and Mercedes-Benzes of my co-
diners, and when he brought the car I got the same snooty treatment that I'd received from the functionaries inside. I would have
changed his tip from a dollar to a quarter if I hadn't had the bill
already in my hand. It was easy to see why people who were broke
to begin with spent their last nickel on expensive cars in Los Angeles. The contempt of a Beverly Hills parking lot jockey was
enough to wither the heartiest individual. I managed to be brave.

Tori was quiet as we wound up Cañon Drive toward Sunset,
then turned west at the gaudy pink stucco bandbox that was the
Beverly Hills Hotel. Then she said, "Do you think Sherwin Mandelker is behind what's happening to my father?"

"Who knows? I've only been on this case a day and a half, you
know."

She lighted one of her evil brown cigarettes and I opened my
window about half an inch so the smoke would be drawn out into
the slipstream. I glanced at her, and decided to plunge in. "There's
something else I don't know," I said. "And I want to. What really
happened to Deke James?"

She didn't answer me right away, but stared out the windshield,
her brow furrowed with thought and worry and indecision, her
lips pursed in what, under more fortuitous circumstances, might
have been a kiss. At last she said, "He had an automobile accident."

"No, he didn't, Tori."

"Yes he did. It was in the papers."

"'Dewey Defeats Truman' was also in the papers. Deke got hurt, all right, but there was no record of any accident. That was a cover-up story. I want to know what really happened."

The tension in her voice made it almost unpleasant. "I told you to ask him."

"I did." She turned to look at me, startled, and I nodded affirmation. "He lied to me, too."

"When did you—?"

"This morning. He gave me the car-crash story. But my assistant checked."

For a moment she looked like a frightened animal in a corner, angry and ready to fight, and then the belligerence went out of her and she took a deep puff of her cigarette. "Jeremy Radisson is a good friend of one of the owners of the Chargers. They both have places in Palm Springs, I guess—it doesn't matter. Anyway, that's how I met Deke. He really rushed me, and when he proposed I said yes. It's too bad, isn't it, the way things are set up that we wind up marrying strangers? Anyway, it was all right for about six months, until football season started. Deke had a bad year. It just sometimes happens to players—no particular reason.

"He was very frustrated about it, and he took out his frustrations on me. At first it wasn't too bad, but by the middle of the season he was hitting me a lot—a couple of times a week."

"Why did you stay? Why does a woman stay with a man who punches her around?"

"I don't know. I got to thinking it was somehow my fault, I was making him do it, I wasn't giving him enough of whatever it was he needed. I took the slaps and punches as something I had coming to me."

"That's a lot of crap, Tori."

"I know that now," she snapped. "But we're talking about a marriage. The old death-do-us-part bit. I didn't want to just walk away when things got less than perfect."

I reached out and took the cigarette from her and puffed on it. Her lipstick was on the filter. Cherry. I gave it back to her.

"The season ended—they didn't make the playoffs. But by that time a pattern had been established, and patterns are hard to break. Deke became more distant—colder, more unreachable. I don't think we made love six times in six months."

I was not proud of myself for being glad about that.

"I also found he was fooling around with a couple of teenage girls who hung out on the beach. Quite a shot to my ego. Then, a year ago spring, when Deke was negotiating a new contract with the team, they threw his lousy season back at him. They offered him a lot less than he thought he was worth, and he had to take it. He'd had the kind of off year that doesn't give a player much leeway. He came home that night in an understandably bad mood, and he split my lip, loosened a tooth, and left me with one eye swollen almost completely shut. I'd had enough, I guess, and the next morning after he'd gone I packed up and left. I went home to my father—it was the only place I could go. It was the first Dad knew Deke had been beating me. He didn't say much then, just that I was welcome to stay as long as I wanted to. He needed a secretary anyway.

"That evening Dad went out. I found later that he'd driven down to Mimosa Beach and waited for Deke in the underground parking area. Dad is awfully strong, and he's used to street fighting. He beat Deke up terribly. And then when Deke was practically unconscious, Dad spread his hands out on the concrete and stomped on them with his boot heels until all the fingers were broken. He said Deke would never hit anyone with those hands again."

She'd said all this in a dead voice, with eyes just as dead staring out through the windshield. "Deke is a proud man. He thought it would be better if the word didn't get out he was beaten so badly by a man thirty years older than he was. So he came up with the accident story. His hands were so badly smashed that his days of catching footballs were over, but because of the publicity he never brought charges against Dad. The divorce was quick and easy because I didn't want anything from him. I just wanted out, and of course, so did he. We spoke on the phone a few times, but I guess he couldn't face me after Dad beat him so badly. I never saw him again."

I was frightened I would get an answer I didn't want to hear, but I had to ask the question anyway. "Do you still love him, Tori?"

"No. I'm not sure I ever really did. There were a lot of men in my life when I was younger. But I think they were more impressed with the Weldon name and the Weldon money than they were with me."

"Hard to believe," I said.

"Deke was different—a celebrity in his own right, and rich at that. I think I married him because he didn't give a damn who Buck Weldon was." She sighed. "That's all ancient history. What's the difference, anyway?"

"Possibly a big difference. Don't you think Deke might hate your father enough to want him dead?" Her eyes widened again, startlingly green in the moonlight. "Deke is an angry man, Tori. I just mentioned Buck's name to him and he went up like a skyrocket." I debated telling her I'd hit him, and concluded it was a bad idea. Every so often I'm capable of a little restraint.

"Deke is no killer," she said. "I'm almost sure."

"Almost isn't good enough."

"Oh, come on! He's just an oversized little boy who never grew up."

"So was Peter Pan, but I don't remember anything about him beating up women. So, just to be on the safe side I'm going to have the police check Deke's alibi for the other night when Marsh Zeidler got shot at."

She started to say something, then changed her mind and instead mumbled, "Suit yourself," and scrunched low in her seat.

It was about then I became aware of the headlights behind me. Because of the twists and turns in Sunset Boulevard I hadn't really noticed them before, and if I had I probably would have ignored them. But he must have been doing more than eighty on a very treacherous road, and when he got to within thirty yards of me he leaned on his horn. I slowed down to let him pass if he was in that much of a rush, but he loomed up behind me instead, still blasting on his horn, and we drove like that for a time, the noise loud enough to cause actual physical vibrations. I tried pulling over to the right to give him passing room, but he would have none of it, and finally, in the middle of a dangerous S-curve, he did pass me, a large, dark, expensive sedan, and he came so close I found myself driving on the shoulder. When he got past he pulled over in front of me and turned his car so that I was completely blocked. I jerked my wheel to the right and drove up onto the hard-packed dirt, braking to a stop about two feet before I hit a tall ivy hedge, putting my right arm out to keep my passenger from sailing through the windscreen. The driver of the sedan got out of his car, and in the glare of my headlights he was easy to recognize in his big, dark suit. Apparently I had made Mr. Mandelker more nervous than I realized, and he'd sent one of his goons to make sure I didn't come around any more.

"Fucking cocksucker, you cut me off!" he bawled. "Whyn't you learn how to fucking drive or get off the fucking road? You almost got us killed, you asshole." He started for my car and I rolled the window down the rest of the way. After all, such eloquence deserves to be heard clearly.

"Get out of that car, motherfucker, I'm going to teach you a lesson."

I sighed a deep sigh that reflected my weariness with the world at that particular moment. It had been a draining day. In the morning I had been manhandled by an ex-professional football player, in the afternoon I had been threatened by a black revolutionary, and now in the evening a designated hitter wanted to rearrange my face. It was a situation that seemed to cry out for firmness. I waited until his meaty paw was about six inches from the door handle and then I reached down under the seat where I keep my .38-caliber Police Special in case of emergencies, and I slid it from its specially designed holster, and raised it to where he could see it, pointed out the car window straight at his genital area, and he suddenly became a statue, frozen in a moment of splendid terror, and even on the dark roadway I could see the color leaving his big, ugly face.

"The way I see it," I told him reasonably, "you have three choices. You can apologize to the lady for your inexcusably coarse and vulgar language and then leave quietly, with dignity. Or you can turn tail and run like the chickenshit I think you are. Or, you can come ahead and put your hand on this car, at which time I am going to shoot off your dick."

His hand wavered. He was actually thinking it over. He backed up a few steps, logic and discretion sinking into his Neanderthal brain, and when he spoke his voice was a lot softer than when he'd been hollering obscenities, and there was fear in the undertone, a kind of obsequious whine I really enjoyed having put there. "Take it easy, buddy. Anybody can make a mistake. Sorry." He put out both hands, and with as much dignity as an orangutan could muster, he moved off crab-fashion to his car. I didn't stir until he had driven away, and then I carefully replaced the piece under the seat.

Tori was rigid with fear and shock, and I smiled at her and reached out to touch her cheek, too late realizing how my hand must smell of gun oil, and I rubbed her cheekbones gently with the backs of my fingers, giving her what reassurance I could, until finally her body relaxed a little. I didn't take my hand away.

"Are you okay?"

She nodded, still unable to talk.

"I'm sorry you had to see that. I shouldn't have brought you along—but I really wanted to be with you tonight. I didn't think things would get rough."

The cigarette she'd been smoking had gone out, and she stubbed it in the ashtray unnecessarily and lighted a fresh one, and it wasn't until after the third deep lungful that she spoke. "Would you really have done it?"

"Shot him? If the alternative was getting beaten senseless, or worse, and God knows what he might have done to you—yes. Not where I said, though. In the knee, maybe. He was no angry motorist. He was sent to get us."

"You've shot people before." It wasn't a question.

"Let's not talk about shooting. Nobody got shot, nobody got hurt, except that ape's dignity. We're here and we're safe. Let's forget it."

"*Can* you that easily?"

"No," I admitted, "but I don't have to dwell on it either. Come on, I'll take you back to your car." I started up the Fiat's motor and backed out onto the asphalt, and we drove quietly for about five minutes.

"I'm really sorry, Tori. I wanted tonight to be special."

As we came in sight of the hotel where she'd left her car, she put her hand on my arm, almost tentatively. "I don't think I can drive home alone just yet," she said.

"All right, honey. You want to stop for a drink?"

She bit her lip and shook her head, and her voice was very small and frightened. "Do you think we could go over to your place for a little bit?"

I had to swallow and clear my throat two or three times before I was even ready to answer. "I think that might be arranged," I said.

"You're a fabulous lover," I said.

We were lying in my bed, my king-size bed that had been so long empty and cold and monastic, and it was good to have someone lovely and warm against me again, lying so close to me that the two of us barely took up the space needed for one, with my left arm under her, supporting her neck, and with her head on my shoulder; she was planting little affectionate kisses on my chest and neck, and I emphasize affectionate because they were not really sexy, at least they were not meant to be, because we had just made love for over an hour, and the sexiness and seductiveness and teasing and tantalizing were over for the moment because we were still panting from the last of it, and there was no come-on in the kisses, just the affection, and it felt monstrous pleasant, as if a persistent and chronic itch had finally been scratched; it felt even better than the sex had (if such a thing were possible, because sex always feels good and sex with someone who obsesses you feels better than that) and I wondered once more at the strange life force that no one had ever been able to explain scientifically, the one so often labeled "chemistry" but that had nothing to do with Bunsen burners and test tubes; that sometimes frightening phenomenon which sends a round-trip jolt of energy coursing between two people when they first meet so that you know from Jump Street that this one is going to be different, this one is going to be a Biggie, it's going to be meaningful and important and good, and so you go for it, even though you know there will be intense pain along with the intense pleasure, and so you buckle up for safety, because you can run from it or deny it's there and say you don't want to get involved right now, but you know it's going to happen anyway just like you know there'll be a day-after-Christmas sale or a prime-time showing of *The Wizard of Oz,* and it's a lot like an airplane ride because there is such anticipation before takeoff and then the elation when you're finally airborne, and then you get comfortable with it because you might as well, you can't change your mind and get off in the middle, so you see it through to its ultimate destination even when it runs into some unexpected turbulence over Salt Lake City.

Once I had undressed her, when we were on top of the blue comforter and I was running my hands all over her incredibly soft body and she was making little whimpering noises, I sensed a holding back, a fear rather than a resistance, and when I finally penetrated the warm wetness of her she arched her body against me as though a duality was at work, as though she wanted to resist me almost as much as she wanted all of me she could get inside her, and though we strained and moved against each other for a long while, she didn't climax until I eased myself off her and out of her, and with my mouth and tongue slowly and teasingly worked my way down over her breasts and stomach, visiting her navel with my tongue, then over the silkiness of her mound and then to the tart, hot wetness beneath, and after a few moments her orgasm came to her suddenly, almost as if it were a surprise, and she writhed and bucked and gave herself to it fully, and after that, after a few moments of cuddling and kissing and stroking each other she climbed astride me and with her hands put me inside her again, and this time there was no hesitation, this time there were no qualms, just a hunger that was equally sharp in both of us, and there was nothing in the world for Tori and me except the places where we were joined, mouths and breasts and hands and loins, and her second climax seemed to last for more than a minute, and then she collapsed on my chest and after a bit we rolled over so that I was once more on the top, and within moments I had reached my own apex, so good that it seemed as though I'd never done it before, so good that it made me wish it was my first time.

Her skin against mine felt good, hot and sweaty and sweet, the warmth and dampness leaving a memory wherever she had touched me, and I paid my compliment to her and she snuggled down against me and we talked low and intense love talk, and then she leaned up on one elbow and kissed me and her hair on my face was fragrant and gossamer, angel hair, and I felt it move down across my chest and belly. When she took me in her mouth there was the hesitation again, but I think it was because she was not really sure what to do. She let her instincts take over, and it was not the practiced expertise learned in the arms of a hundred different lovers, but the shy and excited and nervous experimentation of a woman who wanted to please as she had been pleased.

But the world has a way of intruding on lovers. I had turned on my answering machine so as not to be interrupted, but when the phone rang and the mechanism clicked on I could hear the caller leaving his message, and I recognized Ray Tucek's voice and the urgency in it. I reluctantly reached out and picked the receiver up off the cradle and flicked off the machine so Tori couldn't hear Ray's side of the conversation.

"I'm here, Ray," I said, interrupting the message he was leaving me.

"Well, you'd better get *here,*" he said. "Fast."

The thin warm sheen of perspiration, mine and Tori's, that covered my body all at once turned cold, and what had so recently been fuzzy contentment was now dark and clammy fear. "Why?"

"There's an ambulance in front of the Weldon place with paramedics and cops and the coroner's car. Weldon's okay, though. He was running around on the lawn waving the ambulance down. The only one I saw go in was some blond bimbo with bubbies like the front of a 1953 Studebaker. She came in a LeBaron convertible, and she didn't come out."

"On my way," I said. I hung up and turned to look at Tori. She was small, almost lost, in the acreage of my king-size bed.

"What kind of car does Shelley Gardner drive?"

"Dad bought her a LeBaron last year. Why?"

I bent down and kissed her mouth gently. "Get dressed, honey. There's been an accident. Your father is all right, but I think something has happened to Shelley."

*   *   *

Something *had* happened to Shelley, and if I hadn't shown up on the arm of the daughter of the manor, I wouldn't have found out about it until I read the morning paper, because Lieutenant Jamie Douglas of West Valley LAPD was standing in the doorway of the Weldon house with his arms folded like a wiry ebony eunuch guarding the gates of a seraglio. Except Douglas was no eunuch. A former middleweight boxer, a concerned citizen, a leader of the black community in the San Fernando Valley, and a hell of a cop, I knew him only by reputation. He knew me, though.

"You're Saxon," he said.

I knew that.

"What are you doing here?"

"I'm bringing my date home," I said. "It is Lieutenant Douglas, isn't it?"

"It is."

We were on the porch, and in the driveway was a city ambulance, its orange light hard and assaulting the senses with its relentless flashing, giving a funhouse aspect to everything and everyone in the front yard. Ray Tucek was nowhere in sight, but in the effulgence I was able to pick out paramedics, the police forensic team, the coroner's man, a couple of stringers from the local newspapers, and several plainclothesmen who were easily spotted because of the suits and ties they wore in the informal atmosphere of Southern California. I later found out they were from narcotics and homicide. There was also a large gallery of looky-loos, mostly residents of neighboring houses, several in various stages of nighttime dishabille, and in their worried but eager eyes was the voyeurism that always manifests itself in the bystanders of a tragedy, the undeniable kick of being in on something that could be talked about at the coffee machine tomorrow, and the fear that always comes when Death's footfall is heard on the outer edges of the soul. And relief, too, of course, that it was happening at this house and not next door at their own.

Douglas stepped aside to let us enter the house, and as we did so a mobile unit from Eyewitness News was pulling up to the curb and disgorging a camera crew and a lady reporter with a hardlacquered helmet of ash blond hair and a severe gray suit that made her resemble a middle-management executive with an electronics firm in Ohio. Poor Buck Weldon, he had so wanted to avoid publicity.

He met us in the hall and threw his arms around Tori as if only she could save him from drowning. The sheer weight of him, his arms around her neck, staggered her, and she was practically carrying him as we went through the living room and past a corridor at the end of which the open door of the master suite gaped pitilessly. There were more police inside that bedroom, and bright photographic lights and men shouting orders at each other the way men will do in the course of a day's work even though there was a dead body on the floor. Buck avoided looking in that direction, keeping his head averted the way one tries not to look at a flattened and disemboweled dog at the edge of a freeway. We went into his study and he switched on a green-shaded lamp which added its own Grand Guignol glow to the already grisly proceedings. Buck slumped into his chair with his head thrown back against the darkened leather. The youthful vigor which had been so pronounced at our first meeting was gone, replaced by a drained listlessness made up of equal parts exhaustion and grief. If he took any note of my being out with his daughter or of my bringing her home at one o'clock in the morning, he didn't say anything about it. At this moment the way Tori conducted her sex life was not one of Buck's priorities.

No one said anything for a while. The silence was uncomfortable, especially since we could hear through the closed study door the hordes of police climbing all over the house, but they were removed from us like the sounds from a television set that is on in the corner when no one is watching. I was going to ask questions—I had a lot of them, but one look from Tori changed my mind. She knew her father better than I did, so I shut up and wished I could light a cigarette. Nothing was stopping me, I suppose, but it didn't seem like the thing to do. Finally Buck tilted forward in his chair with a jolt, and rubbed his face with his hand the way Wallace Beery used to, as though he were wiping away something rank and foul. He put both forearms on the edge of his desk and looked at his hands, which he clasped in front of him almost in an attitude of prayer. I guessed correctly that he was now ready to talk about it.

"I don't know," he said to no one in particular. He sounded tired, the kind of tired that is worse than physical exhaustion and worse than lack of sleep. The kind of tired that makes you want to go to sleep and not wake up any more. "I don't know."

Then he looked up at us, first Tori and then me, and said, "She came over at eight—about eight. I asked her to make it kind of a late evening—you know, have dinner before she came—because I was finally getting somewhere on the book. It was no major breakthrough, but my writer's block seemed to be breaking up a little and some stuff was trickling through. Anyway, we had a few drinks. Played a little casino. Watched the news. After the news, about eleven-thirty, we went into the bedroom. I took a shower, and when I came out she'd fixed a couple of lines of coke for us—on her little mirror, you know. So anyway, she takes the first toot, and the next thing I know is she's on the floor having convulsions. She was dead before I could get to the phone." He rubbed his face again. "Jesus Christ, what an awful fucking thing. What a fucking thing to have to see! Jesus Christ!" I thought it ironic that a man so at ease with violent death that he made his living writing about it could be so shaken when confronted with its reality, when life imitated his own art.

"Is that the story you told the police?"

He nodded.

"You do a lot of coke?"

He nodded again.

"How much?"

Pause. "A lot."

I suppose I should have picked up on it when I first met him—the chronic sniffling and rubbing of the nose, the hyper bursts of energy, but then I am pretty naïve about some things. I'm always the last to know who's into whips and boots, who's screwing whom, who's gay. Especially about narcotics I'm a total innocent, even though the world of show business in which I live is awash in hash and cocaine and reds and whites and black beauties and magic mushrooms. I've smoked dope a time or two, but I pride myself that I've never spent a nickel of my own money for it. I only take hits when they pass joints around at a party, and not always then. I guess it just never occurred to me that someone Buck

Weldon's age would be involved in something I usually associated with teenagers or young adults. Silly me.

There was a soft knock at the door and Jamie Douglas stuck his head in without waiting to be asked. "I'm sorry, Mr. Weldon," he said. "They're going to remove—they're taking Miss Gardner away now."

Buck bowed his head, struggling with his emotions, and after holding it in for a few seconds he allowed himself the luxury of tears. Bart Steele would never have cried, and I believe it bothered Buck that in this circumstance he was not as tough as Steele would have been, but he was too overcome with the enormity of it, the finality, the abrupt and unexpected loss, to worry about anything as trivial as his own image. He put his hand over his eyes as if to shade them from bright sunlight, and Tori covered his other hand, lying limp on the desk, with her own. He said to the desktop, "God damn it, she was good people! God damn it!"

I couldn't wait any longer. I took out a cigarette and lighted it, and the sound of my Bic made Tori look up at me. The only sound then was the labored sound of Buck's breathing. Douglas withdrew quietly, and I took another lungful of ill health before I started talking. "Buck," I said as gently as I could, "don't you think it's time to stop playing games and start cooperating with the police?"

He didn't look up. Tori raised her hand to stop me but I was not to be stopped. "Someone tried to run you off a road not too long ago. Marsh Zeidler almost got killed because someone thought he was you. Now Shelley is dead. These aren't characters in a book any more, this isn't one of Bart Steele's cases. Whoever is after you means business."

"What do you want from me?"

"Some help. Some names. The same things the police are going to want. Who would want you dead?"

He shook his head sadly.

"Who would benefit if you were?"

"I don't know. Just my girls." He looked up at me sharply, dangerously, like a fighting bull in the arena. "You aren't saying my girls—?"

"I'm not saying anything, Buck, I'm asking."

All at once he seemed sadder than before. "It isn't my girls," he said.

I looked at Tori. Her face was very tense, her big green eyes slanting and the corners of her mouth pointing at her shoes. "We don't know what happened here tonight," she said, trying to convince herself first, then me. "It could have been a heart attack. It could have been something she had for dinner—botulism or something. It could have been someone was trying to kill *her*. We don't know yet what happened here."

I couldn't deal with her right now, I was busy doing reality. I turned my attention back to Buck. "It's very important, Buck, your life could depend on it, on your leveling with me. You've got to tell me—and the cops—who your enemies are."

He said it almost apologetically, as though it were something to be ashamed of. "I don't have an enemy in the world."

I took another puff but the cigarette tasted lousy, and all of a sudden I realized that in twenty-five years of smoking they had always tasted lousy. I put it out in Buck's already overflowing ashtray. "Well then, Buck," I said, "somebody had better keep a damn close eye on your friends."

Douglas asked me to stay around for a while, and I didn't have a whole lot to occupy me while I was waiting. Buck wanted to sleep on the sofa in his den. "I can't go back in there," he explained about the room in which Shelley had died. He wouldn't even go in for his toothbrush, but sent Tori in for it. While she was inside I wandered out to the living room and over to one of the coroner's men.

"What do you think?" I said.

"About what?"

I made an all-encompassing gesture, taking in the room, the house, the murder, the state of the world.

He eyed me suspiciously. "What are you, writing a book?"

"I might," I said. "How's this: the hero is a smartass on the coroner's staff who solves the crime and gets to screw all the pretty girls." I showed him my PI license. He wasn't impressed.

"What's that supposed to mean?" he said. "That you're my long-lost brother who got carried off by gypsies when we were kids?"

Since he had the nose of a toucan and ears that should have been gray and on the head of an elephant, I considered myself fortunate we were not related. "I'm not on this case officially," I said. That was a lie. "I'm Miss Weldon's date for the evening." That was the truth. "We're engaged." And that was wishful thinking. "So if you could give me some sort of hint—just a crumb—unofficially, of course."

"Yeah?"

"I'd be very grateful. Unofficially."

"Well, unofficially, get fucked, pal. We just got the stiff outa here five minutes ago. The autopsy won't be until tomorrow the earliest."

I sighed and dug into my pocket. Now that Tori and I had made love, I felt badly about spending her money. I made sure no one else was looking, and I pushed the bill into the pocket of the coroner's man's white smock. He looked around quickly, furtively. "Jesus, pal," he said.

"I know the autopsy won't be until tomorrow, but you've been on enough of these mop-ups, you've got to have some idea."

"Use your fuckin' head," he said, tucking the bill further into his pocket until it was out of sight. "The broad's doin' fine till she takes a snort of snow, the next thing you know she checks out. Now, what does that suggest to you?"

"A bad batch of coke?"

"Real bad," he said, taking another look around to make sure we weren't overheard. "Like in laced."

"Laced?"

He was becoming exasperated by my stupidity. "Laced with some other substance. Something that would go up the nose and hit the brain and kill it within seconds."

"Like what?" I persisted.

"Like—strychnine," he said. "Now get outa my face." He walked away from me.

Tori came out of the master bedroom, white and shaken. Even though Shelley Gardner's remains had been taken away, the room vibrated with her death and Tori felt it and had been affected by it. She carried Buck's toothbrush and toothpaste and a clean bath sheet. I followed her back into the den, putting my hand on her back as we went just to let her know I was there, I was near, she had my full support. Buck was sitting on the edge of the couch, which had been made up with a sheet and a blanket and a pillow. He was still wearing the pajamas and bathrobe in which he had met us at the front door. I noticed he needed a shave.

"Buck," I said, "I know how much this has taken out of you—"

"You're starting to be a pain in the ass."

"I'm sorry. I just have to ask you one more question."

He stood up and went to the built-in bar against the wall on the other side of his desk and poured himself a big shot of Wild Turkey without benefit of ice or water or soda. Apparently someone had fetched him another bottle since my visit two nights before, and obviously he'd been at it quite a lot, as there were barely two fingers of bourbon left in the bottle. He drank half the drink down in one gulp before he even looked at me.

"What for?" he said. "Your pal Marsh isn't in any danger, okay? That's all you care about."

"I care about you."

"Why?"

"I like you. I like your writing. And I like your daughter." I looked over at Tori, who flushed. "How are those for reasons?"

"Flimsy, laddie," he said. "But ask your question and then go away."

"Thanks. Who's your coke connection?"

"Huh?"

"Your cocaine dealer. You don't buy it at the corner drugstore."

"I don't buy it at all," he said, and the pain crossed his face as he prepared to speak her name. "Shelley always took care of it." He finished his drink.

"Did she ever mention—?"

"You've asked your one question. Good night, Saxon." He went back over and sat down on the sofa, messing up the bedclothes. "I'm tired and I'm sad and I'd rather cry alone in the dark in here where no one can see me and ask me stupid questions."

Out in the living room there was still a cadre of policemen milling around, but I pretended they weren't there and sat down in an overstuffed chair in front of a rug made out of a leopard, complete with the head intact, the jaws snarling ferociously and the glass eyes staring. The wall-size TV screen looked woeful without a picture on it, and I hardly thought it was appropriate to switch it on, especially since there was nothing likely to be on at this hour of the morning except a plea to help starving Biafran children or an old horror film with George Zucco. Jamie Douglas came over and stood looming in front of me in a manner not designed to give me optimum comfort. I looked up and smiled at him, but he didn't smile back.

"You want to tell me just what you're doing here?" he said. I didn't know Douglas, and until I found out how far I could push him, I decided I'd better suppress my normal tendencies to be a wise-mouth.

"As you know, Lieutenant Douglas, two nights ago someone took a shot at a man named Marshall Zeidler as he was coming out of this house. It so happens his wife works for me, and I came out here to talk to Mr. Weldon, strictly as a favor, all of which I told Lieutenant DiMattia by phone the next day. What I didn't tell him is that I met Mr. Weldon's daughter and invited her out for dinner tonight. She met me in town, in Beverly Hills, I mean, and that's why we came back in separate cars."

"And that's all?"

"That's all."

He made a noise as he sucked some air between his even teeth. Then he matter-of-factly said, "You're lying to me."

"I'm not lying to you."

"Sure you are. You live on the West Side somewhere—the Palisades, is it? Why, if you were in separate cars, did you drive all the way back here? I think someone tipped you off there was something going down here tonight. And I think it was your friend Mr. Raymond Tucek, who's been hanging around here all day in a tan Firebird, and who we made at about ten-fifteen this morning."

I scratched my head. "Well, that's not exactly a lie, Lieutenant. That's just not telling you everything. There is a difference. I haven't told you a lie yet."

"You better not," he said, and all at once what little cordiality had been in his voice was gone, and he spoke in the driving rhythm of the streets, a tough, marble-hard cop getting very spiky, and I got those little prickles on the backs of my hands that come when I get really close to being in deep shit. "You better be a good boy and eat all your spinach and say your prayers at night and stay the hell out of my hair about this or you're going to get a spanking, and I'm not kidding. We understand each other, do we?"

"Yes, sir," I said. I almost meant the sir part.

He said "Good," and walked away from me, making me feel like a car that's just gotten a ticket for parking overtime at a meter. I sat there being in the way, watching everyone from the police and the coroner's office and the press bumping into each other and murmuring that strange baritone masculine murmur you only hear in a crowd of men. The television crews had not been allowed inside the house, but there was a guy from the *Valley Vanguard*, a local newspaper that often had delusions it was the *LA Times*, and he came over to me. He probably spent fourteen hours a day sitting around the squad room at police headquarters and had wandered in here on Jamie Douglas's coattails. He had a pad and pencil in his hand. And he was peering at me with great curiosity.

"Friend of the family," I answered his question.

"You look familiar. You're an actor, aren't you?"

"That doesn't mean I'm not a nice person."

His eyes lit up. I could see him composing the headline for his morning edition, another famous name to add to that of millionaire author-personality Buck Weldon. "I'm sorry," he said, "but I can't place your name."

"Conrad Nagel," I told him. "That's G-E-L. It really pisses me off when people spell it G-L-E."

He wrote it down dutifully and assured me he'd spell it right in the paper, and we chatted for a few minutes about Buck Weldon and then he walked away feeling very self-satisfied at having gotten a celebrity interview and I tried to work up some guilt over the fact that he was just trying to do his job and I had just told him I was an actor who'd been dead for over fifteen years. But guilt always comes pretty hard to me, and I figured an editor would catch the mistake before the paper went to press.

Tori came out of the den, closing the door behind her on a room that had been darkened. I hoped Buck would be able to get a little sleep. Tori looked drawn and tired, and the postcoital glow I'd put on her face a few hours before was gone, replaced by the shadows and lines of tragedy. It disturbed me very much that in her mind, and probably in mine too, our first lovemaking would be inexorably linked to the death of Shelley Gardner, but there wasn't much I could do about it. It wasn't the way I would have written it, but then I don't suppose Shelley would have written it that way either.

"You'd better go," she said.

I stood up and together we walked out to the curb to where I had parked my car. Most of the crowd of curious neighbors had dispersed, and I had parked pretty much away from the center of activity, so we had a certain amount of privacy.

"I'll call you tomorrow," I said.

She just nodded, not looking at me.

"Tori, don't worry. We're going to find out who's doing this. Your father will be all right. Trust me."

She shuddered. I put my arms around her, smelling her hair, aware that her bodily secretions still clung to my own body. I tilted up her chin to kiss her but she pulled away.

"Don't."

"Tory—"

"What happened tonight shouldn't have happened. I was frightened—by that man. I was vulnerable. Let's not talk about it. We're going to keep this on a strictly business basis—"

"Hey," I said, truly stung, "don't make a one-night stand out of me."

"My God, my father's life is in danger! I just can't—I can't even think about you, about us—oh, God damn it!" She started to cry, which made her eyes even more like stars, and she leaned against me, her tears soaking my tie, and I put both arms around her in my most avuncular manner, patting her back gently and trying not to let the closeness of her body against mine arouse me sexually, and that was the toughest job I'd had in a long time.

∘ 7 ∘

Venture City is located in the middle of West Los Angeles, on the site of the backlot of a now-defunct movie studio, but it is a megalopolis unto itself, home to prestigious law firms, brokerage houses, a major TV network, shopping mall, trendy boutiques, a legitimate theater and a triplex movie house and several fast food joints where, at lunchtime, anorexic secretaries eat the salad and search for rich attorneys to marry. Its best-known landmarks are the twin monoliths that stood alone against the skyline until someone built two even uglier side-by-side towers half a block away.

There is one building in Venture City that never seemed to realize in what august company it flourished—and so it tends to attract the fly-by-nights, the guys selling shares in nonexistent Bolivian tin mines, the motion picture companies that never seem to produce a motion picture but raise a certain amount of money with which to do so, hustlers and sharpies and charlatans, highly suspect charitable organizations, all people on the fringe. So many of them had come and gone in this particular high-rise that it became known in some of Los Angeles's wittier circles as the Kellogg Building, because it was so full of flakes. It was in this building that Elliot Knaepple, Buck Weldon's longtime literary agent, maintained a two-room suite of offices he called the Elliot Literary Agency, presumably so named because he figured, with every justification, that no one would ever be able to correctly pronounce Knaepple.

The girl at the front desk was a stunner, overblown and corn-fed and straight out of a small-town beauty contest somewhere in the Midwest, and it wasn't until you noticed that her smile was vapid and there wasn't much going on behind her eyes that you realized she wasn't terribly attractive after all. I told her who I was, which didn't impress her, and she buzzed Knaepple that I was there. He summoned me into his private office. Because of all the things I'd

heard about him, and my natural aversion to agents, I was all prepared not to like Elliot Knaepple, and for once my preparedness
paid off.

Elliot Knaepple was short. Saying a Hollywood agent is short is
almost redundant, because the business of agenting seems to attract
teeny-weenies, most of whom have that aggressive nastiness so
common among men whose stature is Napoleonic. Elliot's height,
combined with his receding hairline, his sharp little nose and myo-
pic eyes and his tiny pursing mouth, gave him the luckless appearance of a ferret, if you can imagine a ferret smoking cork-tipped
cigars and wearing a startling plaid jacket, maroon slacks, maroon
socks and wine-colored Gucci loafers. His manner was that of a
man who thought he was pretty hot stuff. If his legs had been as
long as his ego, Elliot Knaepple might have been the center for the
Boston Celtics.

"I *made* Buck Weldon," he was telling me. "He was running all
over New York with that shitty first book of his and nobody would
give him a look. Nobody would even talk to him. It was dirty. It
was brutal. It was different, and remember those were the
Eisenhower years when everything was bland and nice. But I'm the
one who looked at it and said, this is mean, this is dynamite, this is
gonna go right through the roof. Guys were gonna buy it because it
was dirty, women were gonna buy it because it was a respectable
way to read porno, sickos were gonna buy it for the gore. And I
was right. It went right through the fucking roof. But without me
to spot it for what it was, without me believing in it, Buck would
be selling hardware and writing at night on a yellow pad in the
kitchen."

"You don't think much of Buck as a writer?"

"What do I care if he can write or not? He kept this agency alive
almost single-handed for a lot of years. I still make the bulk of my
bread from him, from that loony Bart Steele. And that gives me the
luxury of being able to represent some really good writers."

"Like?"

"Like I've got a new kid on the best-seller list. An Israeli name of
Avrom Galamb. I represent two senators and a former network
anchorman, and you know the kind of bread those auto-
biographical confessions bring. And Jack Kale, of course."

"You discovered him, too?"

"I was smart enough to read his first manuscript and say that here was going to be one of the giants of American literature. I put my ass on the line to sell him, I stuck with him, and here we are three National Book Awards and a Pulitzer Prize later."

"Why do you suppose he chose you rather than a hundred other literary agents?"

"I dunno. You want to ask him, go find him."

"You've met him?"

"Nope. He sends me a manuscript about once every two years, I send him back checks—less my ten percent. That's our relationship."

"Aren't you curious about him?"

"No—if he wants to live up in the hills like a spazz with a bunch of beaners and rattlesnakes, that's his red wagon. But it's because I handle Kale that senators like Tom Hawke and anchormen like Ron Dwight come to me. Buck Weldon is not respectable. He's just profitable." He blew cigar smoke toward the chandelier. "The kid lives well, Mr. Saxon. I've got a Mercedes. I've got a condo on the Marina peninsula. You see my receptionist out there? She can't type or take shorthand, she never gets a phone message right, and if the truth be told she isn't much of a hump either, but when a chick looks like that, all she has to do is show up. Well, toys like that cost, and the money I make off Buck Weldon allows me to buy them."

"You don't like Buck, do you?"

"What's not to like? Every other year like clockwork I get a Bart Steele, and all I have to do then is make a phone call. I don't have to read the shit."

"I mean as a person."

"I couldn't care less about him as a person, one way or the other. Look, Mr. Saxon, to me everybody is an *X*. If you can make a lot of money with this *X*, you keep it around. If you can't make any money with *that X*, out it goes. So if I have to have a lunch with one of my *Xs* once in a while, no big thing, it doesn't kill me, it's part of the drill. I heard about Shelley, it's too bad, I sent Buck a card, but it was an accident, that's all. Don't make a big deal out of it."

84

"A woman is dead, Mr. Knaepple. How can I not make a big deal out of it?"

"People who do cocaine get hurt."

"Don't you do coke?"

He shook his head. "Poppers. Amies, Amyl nitrate. Just when you're ready to come." He mimed breaking open a popper. He had little tiny hands to go with the rest of him, and I wondered if all his anatomical features were commensurately tiny, and if that might have explained the bored look on the pretty, vacuous face of the receptionist. Watching those small, feminine hands break open a popper in dumbshow while still holding a cork-tipped cigar almost made me laugh, but I managed to hold it to a smile instead. Elliot chose to regard that smile as one of a co-conspirator who also broke open amyl nitrate poppers just when he was ready to come.

"Tell me about the new book," I said.

"Go out and buy it," Elliot Knaepple said. He was a charmer, all right.

"Not that one. The one Buck's writing now."

"It's typical Bart Steele. What more can I tell you?"

"You can tell me if Sherman Mandelker has read it."

Knaepple poked his little ferret face at me, surprised at the turn in the conversation, his eyes becoming smaller than usual. "What do you know about Sherwin Mandelker?"

I took a folded piece of paper out of my pocket and unfolded it carefully. Jo, as usual, had done her homework. I laid the paper on his desk. It was a Xerox copy of an item that had appeared in *Daily Variety* about four weeks before. "I'm sure you've read this, Mr. Knaepple, your name is in it. It says here"—and I turned the paper so that I could read it, even though I knew what it said—"that you recently made a movie deal for three hundred fifty thousand dollars for a new book by your hotshot Israeli writer, Avrom Galamb. You made the deal with Ravensgate Pictures, a production company with a three-picture deal at Mercury Studios, given them by Sherwin Mandelker just before he stepped down as studio head. When Mandelker left Mercury under suspicion of embezzlement he immediately became president of Ravensgate, who just paid you and your writer an awful lot of money. Now, coincidentally, Buck

Weldon's book-in-progress is about a studio head who embezzles money and instead of going to jail gets himself a sweet three-picture deal from that same studio. You are one of the only people in the world who knows the subject of Buck's book, and now someone is trying hard to see that the book is never finished. That's what I know about Sherwin Mandelker."

Elliot Knaepple glared at me, clearly upset. "A guy could get hurt, sticking his nose into places it don't belong," he said in that little munchkin voice of his.

"Not much of a threat," I said, "coming from anyone who'd wear a jacket like that."

He sat up as tall as he could, indignant, and unconsciously brushed at the lapels of his jacket. "Are you implying that I'm a queer?"

"No—I'm implying your taste in clothes sucks, not that you do. I'm also implying you let Mandelker read what Buck wrote about him."

"I let lots of producers read works-in-progress from my writers. It's done all the time."

"Even when that work-in-progress is a roman à clef about that producer?"

"Especially then," he said. "Look, I've got a good business relationship with Sherwin Mandelker. I'm not going to let it get fucked up by an old cokehead who can write about something else. I wanted Mandelker to read it to see if he got mad."

"And if he had?"

"I would have made Buck quit."

"Then since Buck is still at work on the book, may I assume Mandelker did not get mad?"

"No. He thought it was a piece of shit, but he wasn't really mad."

"And he didn't ask you to get Buck to stop?"

"No. He was pissed because Buck and he had lunched a few times and he thought it was a backstab from a friend. That's all he said. That it was a backstabbing piece of shit."

I sat back and crossed my ankles, hoping to take him aback with a change of subject. It worked. "Where do you get your poppers, Mr. Knaepple?"

It startled him, all right. He sputtered before he came up with an answer. "None of your business," he said. It didn't seem to me that answer required sputtering. Then he went on. "That's confidential. Like the confessional. Like a doctor-patient relationship. Look, you're not a cop. I don't have to talk to you."

"Yes, you do," I said. "Because if you don't, I'll go talk to the cops and ask them to ask you. Or better yet," and here I uncrossed my ankles, "I'll take you by your burgundy Guccis and hang you upside-down out the window until you do talk. Now, before I do that, I'll ask you again who your connection is."

He weighed his options, looking around nervously. I even thought for a moment he was going to call for help. "What do you want to know for?"

I stood up leisurely and took a step around the desk toward him.

"Okay okay okay! Jesus Christ!" he said, losing what little color he had. He flipped on the intercom and buzzed Miss Nebraska outside. "Debbie, what's Bert Del Garbino's number?" He jotted it down on a pad that was imprinted FROM THE DESK OF ELLIOT KNAEPPLE and handed it to me. It was a Venture City exchange. I folded it up along with the Xerox from *Variety* and put it in my pocket.

"Is Del Garbino Buck Weldon's pusher too?"

"The fuck do I know? He's a guy, hangs around Venture City. He supplies half the people in this building with whatever they do. I met him in Fast Annie's—the take-out place in the basement."

"Where can I find him?"

He shrugged. "When I need him I call him. You got the number."

"Elliot, what happened to Shelley Gardner was no accident. I got the autopsy report this morning. It was murder—except that it was your best-selling author they were after. Now, is there any other light you can shed on the subject?"

"Why would I want to kill Buck Weldon?"

"Nobody said you did. Did they?"

He ground his cigar out in an expensive onyx ashtray. "You gripe my ass, you know that? You come in here like a one-man gang and you talk tough and throw your weight around and then you practically accuse me of murder."

"I didn't—"

"You think you're pretty buff, don't you? Well, there are ways of taking care of guys like you."

I leaned across the desk so that my face was very close to his. His breath smelled of cigars and Juicy Fruit gum. "When you figure out one of those ways," I said, "make sure you bring somebody with you."

I went down to the bank of phones in the lobby and called Jo to have her track down an address for Bert Del Garbino. I'm not sure why I wanted to talk to him—in a city the size of Los Angeles it was inconceivable that he would be Buck Weldon's friendly neighborhood pusher. But I thought he might be able to tell me something that might help me track down that batch of laced cocaine. Then I called Professor Kullander at UCLA. He seemed surprised to hear from me.

"I read about Miss Gardner in the paper," he said. "Is that part of your investigation too?"

"Let's just say I'm making it my business."

"I assumed the police would be taking things over from here."

"The police are in the business of solving crimes," I said. "I'm more into crime prevention."

"A worthy ambition, if often hopeless. I applaud you. Now, how may I help you?"

"Have you ever read anything by a young Israeli named Avrom Galamb?"

"Half a novel."

"What?"

"He's only written one, and I was able to get through only half of it before losing interest. Perhaps a bit less than half."

"It wasn't good?"

"I don't know about good. It was slick, it was commercial, written with an eye to the best-seller list and a movie deal, both of which were achieved, I understand. But he's not a—writer."

"Not like Jack Kale."

"N-no," Kullander said, "not even the same species as Jack Kale."

"You make it sound as though writing a best-seller is something shameful."

"Not at all. Remember, Mr. Saxon, I'm an academic. I approach writing on its literary merit alone. Hemingway, Steinbeck, Saul Bellow—they wrote best-sellers, too. But if you want to talk commercial, if you want to talk sales charts and paperback reprints, you must see an agent or a publisher or a retailer."

"You think Jack Kale's writing is strictly literary?"

"It's both. That's what makes him one of the greats. You see, he tells stories that fascinate everyone, stories of dark lusts and buried secrets, and that makes people buy the books. But he also writes with such translucence, such clarity, sometimes the words are so sharp they hurt."

"Do you think Buck Weldon's writing is both?"

"Of course I do," Kullander said with a hesitation that was barely noticeable. "Within the rather stringent limits of the genre, naturally."

"What do you suppose Weldon's work would be like if he didn't stay within those limits?"

"You mean, if he chose to write other than about macho private eyes? I suppose he would be a major writer. I'm not sure I'm following you, Mr. Saxon. Or if I understand precisely what you're after."

"I just wanted your opinion on Avrom Galamb, and I got it. I thank you for your time, Professor."

I wasn't sure why I had called him myself, except that something was nagging me deep inside my frontal lobes. I didn't know where I was heading with this investigation and I somehow figured Kullander could help me with it. He was certainly the only person I'd talked to who wasn't hostile, and maybe I just needed a few strokes, or maybe it was because, like Buck, I enjoyed the way Kullander's mind worked. I called Jo back and she told me that Bert Del Garbino's number rang in an office in the very building where I now stood, and was listed as belonging to D. G. Enterprises. The directory board by the elevators told me D. G. Enterprises was in Suite 304.

Suite 304 was a one-room office, even smaller than Knaepple's, and Bert Del Garbino turned out to be smaller than Knaepple, too, with a whiny East Bronx accent like Dustin Hoffman's in *Midnight Cowboy*.

"I'm a friend of Elliot Knaepple's," I started, but he cut me off with an angry gesture.

"Without the birdshit," he said. "You're no friend of Elliot's because he just called me and told me he'd fingered me."

"I'm not a cop," I said.

"I don't care if you're the archangel Michael, I don't talk without my lawyer."

"A friend of mine got hold of a bad batch of coke," I explained. "I'm just trying to find out where it came from."

"Not here," Del Garbino said with righteous outrage. "I haven't moved any coke in months. I do mostly pharmaceuticals here anyway. Uppers, downers, ludes, poppers. Coke and horse and acid and shit like that, it's too much trouble and it's too dangerous."

"Well, who do you know that does move coke?"

He laughed in my face. "You must think I'm some dumb son of a bitch. I don't name names—that's how I stay healthy. You can threaten Knaepple, but you don't scare me half as much as the people you want me to blow the whistle on. They don't fuck around, they play hardball. So as far as I'm concerned you can go piss up a rope."

I smiled. I hadn't heard that one in a long time. If nothing else the little bastard was refreshing in his candor. "Okay, Bert," I said, "I'm not looking to get you hurt, or busted, either. Pretend I'm a stranger in town looking for a toot. Where would you suggest I go?"

"My mother told me never to talk to strangers."

"Come on, Bert, a hint."

"Around here? You're eight blocks from UCLA, that's where I'd go."

"Where at UCLA?"

"Well, not the fucking Poli Sci Department. There's a little bar just off campus, on Gayley. They call it Snuffy's. Inventive, huh? Anyway, it's out by the movie theaters someplace. I never go in there. Guys that hang out in Snuffy's generally don't have any nasal passages left."

"Appreciate it, Bert," I told him. I did. It was typical of me not to know where to score drugs. It's a lucky thing I didn't live during prohibition—I'd have died of thirst.

Snuffy's Bar was easy to find in Westwood Village. It was small and dark and smelled of stale beer and staler tobacco smoke, with *essence de urinal* thrown in for good measure. I imagine one with a keener nose than mine would have detected the sickly sweet odor of cannabis as well. There was an awful type of music known as "ska" playing on the jukebox. The room was not quite half full, and there were no females in evidence anywhere except for two bare-breasted lovelies painted on black velvet over the bar. The bartender, who may or may not have been Snuffy himself, was well into his fifties and had nicotine stains on all his fingers and a permanent squint in his left eye from the lighted cigarette that apparently lived in the corner of his mouth. Saving his presence I was the oldest person in the bar by at least fifteen years, which may have accounted for the cessation of all talk when I stepped through the open doorway. I felt like the Ringo Kid walking into the Lordsburg Saloon in *Stagecoach*.

I went to the bar and ordered a Heineken. Snuffy gave it to me without comment, but he stood there and looked at me while I took my first few sips. He didn't say anything, he just looked. "This hits the spot," I said. He didn't answer me. I took another swallow. "Not much of a kick, though." He didn't answer me. "Kind of tame." He didn't answer me. "You're a regular jabberjaws, aren't you?" I said.

"Lemme save you some time," Snuffy said. "You're gonna ask me if I know where you can get something with a little more pizzazz to it. I'm gonna say I don't know what you're talking about. You're gonna say 'You know, I wanna score some drugs.' I'm gonna say that this is a saloon—you want drugs, you should go to the drugstore. You're not gonna believe me and we're gonna shoot some shit for about ten minutes, but you're not gonna get anything from me because I know you're a cop, I can smell it all over you, I don't care how pretty you are. You want another beer, it's a buck and a half. You wanna score dope, you're in the wrong store. You want conversation, call the suicide hot line."

I finished my beer with one long pull. "Snuffy," I told him, "you just blew your tip."

I swung off the bar stool and started across the room to the door. A tall, muscular figure appeared in the doorway, silhouetting his trapezoidal physique and fuzzy Afro hairdo against the light from outside. He saw me and stopped almost in midstride.

"Hello, Abdul," I said. "Long time no see."

"Shit," he breathed.

"That's no way to talk."

"What the fuck you doin' here, man?"

"Same thing the fuck you're doing here, man. I just came in for a drink."

"Bullshit," he said.

"If you say so."

"Why you hassling me, man? I'm nothing to you."

"I'm not hassling you, Abdul. I didn't even know you'd be here. You've got a bad case of paranoia."

"Whassat?"

"Oh, knock off the jive-ass crap, Abdul, you're a college student. You can talk as well as I can."

"I can hit harder," he said.

"Why are you hostile, Abdul?" I said. "I've tried to be nice—"

"You gonna get socked, is what you are."

"Ease off—"

"Don't walk up, man. Be cool."

"I have no idea what you mean, Abdul, but I wouldn't think of it. Have a nice day." He was still in the doorway and I had to turn my body to the side to pass him. He didn't give a millimeter. My skin crawled from the animosity his body gave off, and it remained crawly as he watched me go down the sidewalk. It occurred to me that Abdul was a lot more antagonistic to me than the situation with Valerie warranted, and I wondered if one of these days I was going to have to find out why.

Jeremy Radisson was one of the few publishers who operated out of Los Angeles rather than New York or Boston or Philadelphia, and I was rather thankful for it. It made my job a lot easier. However, when I called his office they told me he was in Palm Springs for the rest of the week. They wouldn't give me the number down there, so I called Tori Weldon for it.

After she'd looked the number up for me I said, "Want to take a ride to Palm Springs?"

"You know I can't leave Dad. You even told me not to."

"I know," I said, remembering. "It just would have made a dreary trip something really special, that's all."

She didn't say anything.

"I need to talk to Buck again."

"No."

"Why not?"

"He's still very shaken up. He can't see anyone."

"He's going to have to see me."

"Why?"

"Because I'm trying to save his life, Tori."

I heard her exhaling a lungful of smoke, and was picturing her sensuous mouth around that awful brown cigarette. Then she said grudgingly, "All right."

"I'll be out after dinner," I told her. "Around eight." And then I said, "I'm not coming out *just* to see Buck, you know," and I hung up before she could give me any shit about it.

Driving northward that evening through the Sepulveda Pass on the San Diego Freeway, I could see the broad carpet of lights of the San Fernando Valley winking sickly through the yellow smog, as though someone had taken a wide-angle photograph of the Valley with a piece of wet yellow toilet paper over the lens. The storm of a few nights before had gone east to Arizona, leaving in its stead a cold, damp dinginess that felt like waking up with a hangover in a cheap downtown hotel. Traffic was light and I made good time out to Verdant Hills.

Tori and Buck and I sat in the living room, because Buck had converted his study into a bedroom, closing off the master suite where Shelley had died like the forbidden wing at Manderley. Buck was still drinking his Wild Turkey, and from his slightly slurred speech I guessed he had been at it pretty steadily all day. Tori and I were sipping on her marvelous chicory coffee and trying hard not to look at one another.

Buck was staring into the depths of his drink, perhaps divining the future from the ice-cube patterns. "This stinks," he was saying. "This is really lousy." He looked up at me. "I'm too old for this shit, Saxon, too old to start over. To be alone." He sucked at his drink. "I wish you'd get off my back."

"I'm trying to help you."

"Who are you? Jesus Christ? Can you raise the dead? Well, then, you can't help me, so get off the pot."

"Buck, where did Shelley score her cocaine?"

"I told you before that I didn't know."

"Did you give her the money for it?"

"I gave her money the first of every month, like an allowance. A big one. What she did with it was up to her. She could spend it on booze, dope, clothes, going to the movies. It was her money."

"Did she get you into doing coke or did you get her?"

"What's the difference?"

"Just curious."

"Then none of your business." He got up and freshened his drink and then apparently forgot it was none of my business because he answered me anyway. "You damn kids," he said, ignoring my gray hair, "you think you discovered drugs. Back in the forties and fifties we were smoking shit before it got trendy. Back when people thought you smoke one joint and suddenly you're a dope fiend. You don't hear that much any more," he mused. "Dope fiend. I think it's one of those expressions I miss." He went and sat back down. "I did coke years ago—not a lot. I've always been more of a drunk than a druggie. Some speed when I needed it. Never downers. The whole world's a downer, whaddya need pills for that for?"

Tori said, "Dad, have some coffee," but he waved her away.

"When I met Shelley she'd been around this town for a while, been into a lot of stuff. And she liked doing blow. After a while I just assumed she was going to buy it. I got into it a lot—more than I should have, I guess. But I do lots of things more than I should."

"And you didn't know where she was getting it? You never thought to ask?"

"She could have scored it at the Methodist church for all I know. Why should I give a damn where she was getting it?" He stood and paced, agitated. "Was I supposed to know someone was going to kill her?"

Tori glared at me. "Can't this wait?"

"Tori," I said, "there's a killer out there. If we could get him to wait, then we could. But we can't, so I need some answers."

"I don't have any goddamn answers!" Buck thundered. His eyes were moist. It could have been from the booze, and it could have been from the chain-smoking, but I believe he was trying hard not to cry. He added softly, "I guess I never did have all the answers."

Tori said, "That's enough, now. Dad is very tired. You'll have to do this some other time." She stood up, looking pointedly at me, waiting for me to get to my feet. I took a last gulp of the coffee and went toward the door.

"Buck," I said before I left, "if you can think of *anything* . . ."

He just waved his glass at me in dismissal. If I had ever seen a man in the doldrums, it was Buck Weldon.

Tori walked me out to the front of the house. "Can't you see the pain he's in?"

"Can't you see the danger he's in?"

"Danger of cracking, I'd say."

I sighed. "Okay, I'll let him alone if I can. But I need you to do one thing for me."

"What?"

"Get me a key to Shelley's apartment."

"Why?"

"I don't know, I'd just like to take a look around."

"For what?"

"Tori, if I knew for what, I wouldn't have to look for it."

She frowned. "He keeps it on his key ring. I'll have to sneak it—he'd never give it to you. He won't like the idea of your pawing through her things."

"I'm not a lingerie freak," I said testily. Then I took her in my arms and said, "Unless it's yours," and tried to kiss her. She remained passive in my arms. It was not a terrific kiss.

"What's wrong?"

"I meant what I said. We made a bad mistake last night. Let's not make any others."

"It wasn't a mistake. Don't you know how much I care about you? Can't you tell? You think I do this with all the girls?"

"I—just don't push me, okay?" With her free hand she disengaged my fingers from her arm and went back into the house, and the door closed with a bit more force than I thought was absolutely necessary.

I stood there in the driveway feeling foolish, feeling rejected, feeling bereaved, feeling bad about myself and a little angry, too. I can usually deal with rejection as long as I understand it, but when I don't understand it's a bitter pill to have to swallow, and where I swallowed it there was a big hollow empty place inside me, and that empty hollow made my heart sound like a big bass drum in an echo chamber. I walked slowly down the driveway and then across, the street to where I'd parked my car. If they'd had any class at all they'd have supplied an empty tin can for me to kick.

On the drive down to Palm Springs the mountains got in the way of Los Angeles radio reception, so my choices were a syrupy "elevator music" station playing Christmas songs, some country and western, or what the kids call "heavy metal," featuring groups I'd never heard of singing unintelligible songs. I flicked off the radio and concentrated on my own thoughts, through which Tori Weldon romped and played. When I wasn't dwelling on her I was thinking about all the people I'd met on the Weldon case, about the precocious Valerie and the ubiquitous Abdul; about golden Deke James and the vulture's claws where his hands used to be; about Sherwin Mandelker and his eight-hundred-dollar suit and his goons and his entourage; about Elliot Knaepple and his burgundy ensemble; and about what I was going to say when I reached the hilltop home of Jeremy Radisson, publisher. Offhand I couldn't think of much, and I wasn't sure why I was going to all the trouble of making the trip, except that I was being paid and it was an avenue down which I had not yet traveled, and the path you don't follow is the one that often leads out of the woods. It certainly wasn't because I loved the thought of spending a day in Palm Springs.

Palm Springs, once fabled as the playground of the stars and now boasting streets named after Bob Hope and Frank Sinatra, lies some 130 miles southeast of Los Angeles, and seems to be populated mostly by past-middle-age matrons with burnished leathery brown skin who wear pastel-colored tennis outfits and sun visors as they swoop down like birds of prey on the overpriced shops and boutiques of Palm Canyon Drive, and by their husbands, little old men in Adidas jogging suits who walk around slowly with their hands clasped behind their backs and tell anyone who will listen how it was before they retired from the chocolate distribution business. Geared for the spoiled rich and attracting the retired and aimless, Palm Springs has become God's Waiting Room. The city makes little obeisance to the Christmas season save for a few chaser lights in the windows of the more tourist-oriented souvenir and curio shops. Perhaps that is due to the large Jewish population, but I tend to think it's because everyone in Palm Springs is just too rich to give a shit about Christmas.

I stopped at a Unocal station built hard by the foot of the mountain that looms over the town like a rocky *dueña,* and got directions. It seemed everything in Palm Springs not named after a movie star or a country club was called Tahquitz and resolutely pronounced "Taco-witz" by the locals. Following the pump jockey's instructions I wound my way up a steep incline until I found myself with a breathtaking view of Palm Springs, Cathedral City and Palm Desert, taking deeper breaths because the air up there was so thin. This was the mountain eyrie of Jeremy Radisson, built, no doubt, on the foundation of the blood-spattered criminals mowed down in the course of duty by Bart Steele.

A maid showed me out to the terrace. It was a cool winter morning in the desert, even more so three thousand feet up, but the sun blessed and warmed all that it touched, and on Jeremy Radisson's terrace it had a pretty clear shot at touching everything. The house was built into the side of the mountain, and the terrace cantilevered out into space, its steel-and-concrete foundation sunk into the side of the rock a good hundred feet to support the heavy flagstone decking the size of a major league infield that attached the terrace to the house proper. The view took in about 300 of the 360 degrees available, which was about all there was to see of the entire desert between Palm Springs and Indio, all of it sand-tan and dust-yellow with an occasional splash of color where someone had planted a date palm orchard or constructed a country club.

Jeremy Radisson was drinking coffee from a Wedgwood coffee service, seated at a glass-topped table big enough to have accommodated Willie Mosconi and Minnesota Fats in a friendly game. From his vantage point near the railing Radisson could get his money's worth of the view. There were several manuscripts atop the table as well as one on his lap, open, which he put aside as he stood to greet me. If you were to look in the dictionary under "distinguished" there would probably be a picture of Jeremy Radisson as illustration. In his early sixties, he managed even in white cords and a Pierre Cardin shirt and sky-blue cashmere sweater to look like Bennett Cerf. He gestured me into a chair at the table, not too far from his own to be out of earshot, and poured me some coffee. I could tell he felt pretty good and democratic about roughing it and pouring the coffee himself when he could just as easily have called the maid. When he took off his glasses there were deep red indentations etched into the sides of his nose, indicating that he wore the glasses to read the many manuscripts that were submitted to his office each week. His eyes were watery blue and he rubbed them a lot.

"I have to tell you, Mr. Saxon, that I didn't particularly want to talk to you. I'm only doing so because Tori Weldon asked me to. Cocaine and murder and private investigators are just not part of my world."

"I'll try to be as brief as I as I can, Mr. Radisson," I said. His crack annoyed me, but then sometimes I know I'm a bit thin-skinned, and realizing that, I make allowances for people. "I believe that someone is trying to kill Buck Weldon. I think they killed Shelley Gardner by mistake and that they will try again. I'm talking to everyone who is close to Buck to see if I can get some ideas about preventing this someone from doing what he wants."

"How can I possibly help you?"

"By telling me everything you can about Buck. You've known him almost as long as anyone—"

He put up an immaculately manicured hand. "Mr. Saxon," he said, "Buck Weldon is not my friend. I publish his books and make a great deal of money from doing so. We meet socially on occasion, and for business purposes whenever feasible, and that's all. I can't tell you what time Buck writes and what time he plays, or who he does either with, if that's what you're getting at. I would think that his daughter could have supplied that information."

"How often does Buck do a Bart Steele book?"

"His pattern has been one every two years or so."

"Is that about standard?"

"For whom? Erle Stanley Gardner used to grind out Perry Masons and Donald Lam and Bertha Cools every six weeks. John D. MacDonald's output was voluminous. Other writers take two months agonizing over a paragraph. What's standard for one is not necessarily standard for the other."

"Don't mystery writers usually work a bit faster?"

"I suppose," Radisson said. "I think Buck takes time off in between to enjoy himself."

"Tori says he writes all the time."

"Then perhaps he's writing his memoirs."

"She told me you've read the first hundred pages of his new book."

"Yes, I did."

"What did you think?"

His eyebrows went up an inch or two. "I think it will make a lot of money."

"That's all?"

"I was concerned at first. There is no question that the manuscript is based on a true story that happened in the film industry. I dislike lawsuits. They leave my otherwise orderly life in a state of disarray. But I determined that there was nothing libelous in the book, at least not so far, and told Buck to go ahead with it, but be careful."

"Why? If there was no libel?"

"Mr. Saxon, you are, I believe, one of those very fortunate people who doesn't care much about money. You like it, and you'll do what you have to to get it, enough to live on for a while, but you are not obsessed with the making of it and keeping of it like so many of us are. Those of us whose orientation is capitalistic are forced by circumstances to be pragmatic. The harsh realities of publishing are that we make an awful lot of money selling our fictional properties to motion pictures or television. I am not anxious to alienate anyone influential or powerful in the film industry, and not just because of Buck Weldon. I could be seriously jeopardizing the future earning power of all the authors on our list."

"Are you aware that Sherwin Mandelker has read the manuscript as well?"

He started at the name. "You've done some work on this, Mr. Saxon."

"I've even talked to Mandelker. Did you know he's read it?"

"I authorized Elliot Knaepple to send it to him, yes."

"And?"

"Mandelker's attitude was sticks-and-stones. I breathed a lot easier, I can tell you."

"Buck is your biggest author, is he not, Mr. Radisson?"

"In terms of sales, yes."

"Meaning in terms of something else, no?"

"We publish at least twenty fiction titles each year. There are a lot of fine writers on our list, nonfiction as well as fiction. We were even able to publish an anthology of contemporary poetry two years ago. Of course, it didn't make us any money. As a matter of fact we took a hosing on it. But we have some really first-rate literary people."

"Like Avrom Galamb?"

"We've done quite well with Avrom."

"Senator Tom Hawke?"

"Yes."

"Jack V. Kale?"

"Mmm-hmm."

"The DBS anchorman, Ron Dwight?"

"What is the point of all this?"

"Aren't they all represented by Elliot Knaepple?"

"Yes, they are, those that you mentioned. Are you suggesting there is something wrong with that?"

"Not at all. Do you mind if I smoke?"

He waved his permission and I lighted up. The tobacco burned quickly in the thin mountain air and after four puffs I was ready to quit. My impulse was to flip it out over the railing, just to see how many hundred feet it would fall, but memories of Smokey the Bear made me grind it out where I was supposed to.

Radisson said, "I don't see where any of my other clients have anything to do with Buck, or any attempt on Buck's life."

"I'm not sure there is any," I said, "but I'd be remiss in my job if I didn't ask a lot of questions."

"Your questions don't seem to be going anywhere."

"I'm afraid you'll have to let me be the judge of that, Mr. Radisson. I'd think you'd be worried about Buck, too—your top author and all."

"I am. But I don't see the point of dragging my other authors and their agents into—"

"Nobody's dragging anybody anywhere. We're on the same side here."

Radisson began stuffing a briar pipe with aromatic tobacco that I could smell even before he put flame to it. A rich smell. I believe that most pipe smokers use the elaborate preparations they must go through to buy themselves some thinking time. I am sure that's what Radisson was doing while he fooled with the pipe. He said finally, "I might as well tell you this, because you're going to find out anyway. Buck Weldon is planning to sue me."

I blinked. Life was certainly full of surprises.

"With *Avenging Angel* there was some discrepancy between my sales records and what Buck feels was due him."

"How much is the lawsuit?"

"The lawyers are still talking, but you can figure in the neighborhood of half a million dollars."

"That's an expensive neighborhood."

"Indeed." He puffed. He wriggled a bit under my gaze.

Finally I said, "Can I ask you something off the record?" He nodded. "If you go to court with it, will you win?"

The blue pipe smoke wafted out across the valley. About a mile away a hawk circled. Radisson considered my question for quite a while. Then he said, "No. No chance of it. We'll have to settle out of court. Now, that's between you and me." He looked at me. "Does that make me a suspect or something?"

"You always have been, Mr. Radisson."

By the time I arrived back at my little rump-sprung office in Hollywood I had a headache of heroic proportions from driving due west into the sun all afternoon, and there was a big orange sphere that seemed permanently grafted onto my eyeballs, even though it was six o'clock and winter-dark when I pulled into my parking place. I knew I could have picked up my messages by phone, and that Jo would be long gone, but I needed to sit and have a quiet drink and let my spinal column heal from the bumps and jars of the road.

I walked up the stairs to the second floor and unlocked my office door. It was not the typical Alan Ladd "private eye" office with gold leaf lettering stenciled on opaque glass, and there was no swinging wooden gate separating the outer office from the inner. Those films were of the forties and they didn't build offices like that any more. Mine had carpets and fluorescent lighting, and the door was solid with a discreet white-on-black nameplate affixed to it with Super Glue, and inside was a large outer office and two inner offices plus a supply room which housed the Xerox machine and the coffee pot. I used to share the place, and Jo's services, with an automobile insurance broker, but he had moved out a year ago because he felt the transvestite bar downstairs and the private eye next door was bad for his image. I didn't care. My image couldn't have been damaged if I'd shared office space with an abattoir.

All the lights were off, and that should have been the tip-off. Since the building paid for the utilities we almost always left the lights on for the cleaning crew, who usually showed up after eight and who, in turn, were simply too indolent to turn them off again when they left. But the office was dark and the incongruity didn't hit me until milliseconds before something else did, across the back of my neck, and I turned a pretty good forward somersault with a tuck before remaining conscious became too much trouble for me and I slipped into a big dark hollow full of glaring orange setting suns that hurt my eyes but didn't really explain the throbbing pain at the base of my skull, right across that place where, in the days of short haircuts, the barber used to buzz with his electric clippers.

I don't know how long I was out, but the first thing I saw, when the glue on my eyelids became unstuck, was the fluorescent light on the ceiling burning down on me. I was lying on the couch in my inner office, and behind my desk, in my chair, was an intruder.

It took me a while to focus on him—for a few moments all I could see was dark bulk. But when the fog lifted I recognized him as Sherwin Mandelker's bully boy from the encounter on Sunset Boulevard. My gun was still in the car, and my other one was locked up tight in the office safe, which meant that he couldn't get it but I couldn't either. It was not feasible to ask him to wait while I fumbled around with the combination. So I tried to sit up, and he came around from behind my desk to the sofa and said, "Real slow, wise-ass, and don't get cute."

Again, cute. You too, brute? I sat up slowly, rubbing the back of my neck. "Who let you in?" I croaked.

He took a long, thin lock pick out of his pocket. I recognized the type—I carried one myself at times. He leaned back with his buttocks against the front edge of the desk, and I calculated what it would require to take him out. It was more than I had. I settled for leaning back on the sofa. "You're going to a lot of trouble just to get even, aren't you?"

"Shut up," he said.

I shut up. He shut up. We looked at each other in a most unloving way, and the moments of my life were ticking by too quickly for my taste. I said, "What's up?"

"You'll find out."

"Give me a hint."

"Look, fuckface, I'd just as soon use you for my heavy-bag workout, so don't get me pissed off. Just put a lid on it."

I did, but not before I said, feeling very much like a six-year-old trying to stretch his bedtime, "Can I have a drink of water?"

"No."

It wasn't until he refused my request that I realized just how much I wanted a drink of water. The trip had been long and dusty, my head was pounding like a Louis Bellson solo, and my mouth felt as though the Yugoslavian army had used it for close-order drill practice. But I took his advice to put a lid on it, and we sat there like two strangers in a stalled elevator for about fifteen minutes until I heard the outer door open and then close. After a moment Sherwin Mandelker appeared in the doorway. He was wearing gray slacks and a blue blazer, and his brilliant white shirt was open at the neck, two buttons' worth, revealing a heavy gold chain with a large gold *chai* at the end of it. The light glinted off his glasses.

"Where have you been, Mr. Saxon?" he said. "George here has been waiting for you for hours."

"I stopped to talk with Huckleberry Finn."

He smiled without amusement. "I'm sure your devastating sense of humor brings you a certain amount of success with the lady barflies at the Ginger Man, but it's only going to get you into trouble here. However, that question was really rhetorical; my subsequent ones will not be, and I suggest that you answer them with a minimum of amusing embellishment."

"Are you sure I have the answers?"

He moved over next to George and leaned against the desk. Standing together the two of them looked like Great Claus and Little Claus. "You'd better." He took a cigarette out of a gold case and George lighted it for him.

"You disturbed me at dinner the other night. You upset me and embarrassed me in front of my friends. I want to know why."

"How about if I simply apologize for my rudeness?"

"I've told you I don't like shakedowns. That's why I sent George to you after dinner—to emphasize my point. Of course I had no idea you went around so well protected."

"Yeah, well, it's a jungle out there."

"I'd like to know exactly what it is you wanted."

"I didn't want anything, Mr. Mandelker, except a few minutes' conversation. I got that."

"I'm something of a public figure, Mr. Saxon. Now that Buck Weldon's lady friend has had that rather bizarre accident, I don't particularly care to have my name linked with his. Now, I want to know what your angle is."

"I have no angle."

"I'll ask you again, Saxon, and then I'll have George ask you."

"I have no angle, and I have no answers for you. I'm working on an investigation that has to do with Mr. Weldon, and for the rest, I have to plead confidentiality."

Mandelker sighed and nodded to George. George came up off the side of the desk and pulled me from the sofa by the front of my shirt. With his other hand he punched me in the gut. Hard. I would have gone down if he hadn't had hold of me—I had very little air left in my body. The second punch took care of the remainder. He dropped me back down on the sofa like a sack of garbage and I fell over sideways, drawing my legs up and hugging them to my stomach. For a moment it was like a nightmare where you want to yell but somehow you can't, except that instead of being unable to yell I was having a lot of trouble inhaling. From a long way off, through an echoey tunnel, I heard George saying, "Not so fuckin' tough without your piece, are you?"

It probably didn't take the several hours it felt like for me to sit up again; about a minute would probably be a closer estimate. I was too busy trying to gulp oxygen to look at the sweep hand of my watch. When I finally was back among the land of the more-or-less normal Mandelker said, "I'm a very influential and powerful man, Saxon, and because of that I have a lot of enemies, some I don't even know about. I want to find out if you're one of them, or if you're working for one of them. So I'm going to ask you again."

My stomach lining felt wadded up like a used paper napkin, and when my voice came out of my body it sounded like a bad impressionist doing Lionel Barrymore. "I told you—I'm not trying to get you. I'm investigating Buck Weldon."

This time George went for the head. The blow, open-handed, landed on my left temple, and felt as if someone had just embedded a javelin into my cerebellum. The force of the slap knocked me completely off the sofa and onto the floor, face down. From the stale smell of the carpeting I realized the cleaning crew was just as cavalier about vacuuming as they were about turning out the lights. I lay there listening to the Balinese temple gongs going off in my head, and so was unprepared for the kick that caught me in the kidney. It was as close as I'd come to wetting my pants since I was three. After a respectful interval I heard Mandelker say, "This is really very stupid of you. If I let George start to work on your face, your future acting career will be limited to creature movies."

From my excellent vantage point flat on my face I could see out the doorway of my office into the big outer room and the door to the hall, and through the crack beneath it I noticed the shadow of two feet stopping at the door. I didn't know who it was, of course. It may have been Mandelker's other bodyguard, but that didn't really matter because I was already overmatched, and if it were anyone else at all I was ahead of the game. I knew the door was unlocked—George had left it that way for Mandelker to enter. I saw the knob begin to turn and I groaned loudly to cover the sound of the door opening. It also warned the new visitor that all was not peaceful within, and he or she stopped for a moment and listened, door ajar. Mandelker said, "Be smart, Saxon. Get up on your feet and start talking to me."

The front door opened a little bit more and the bulky figure of Ray Tucek stood there, wearing a fleece-lined leather vest and jeans tucked into cowboy boots, and from the carpet my eyes met his in complete understanding and he eased the door closed so there was no sound to announce his presence. He started walking toward the inner office where we were, as close to tiptoeing as his high-heeled Western boots would allow, and I said to Mandelker, "Okay, no more. No more," and I began pulling myself up with the aid of the sofa, and when my feet were under my weight and I was still doubled over, I bent my knees and launched myself at George's stomach, head first, and because he wasn't expecting it at all—had I not had reinforcement in the next room it would have been one of the classically stupid moves of all time—it took his breath away and sent him stumbling back toward the doorway into the tender ministrations of Ray Tucek, who exerted himself only to the tune of one karate chop to the side of George's neck. The blow barely traveled four inches but the impact could have been heard way down in Torrance, and George dropped where he stood, not to rise again for a while. It all went down so fast Mandelker had no time to react, still leaning against the front edge of my desk with a cigarette elegantly held between two manicured fingers, staring at Ray as though he'd dropped in from a galaxy far away.

"Good evening, Raymond," I said, getting to my feet. "I believe you know Mr. Mandelker."

"Only by reputation," Ray said. "What's going on here?"

"Ray has some questions, Mr. Mandelker. I'll ask you once and then I'll have Ray ask you."

He delicately flicked his cigarette ash into my dirty ashtray. "That won't be necessary," he said. He was obviously a hell of a lot smarter than I was.

106

"Good." I stepped over George and sat down on the sofa. I was sick to my stomach, I could still feel the impact of George's hand tingling on the side of my head, and there was an ache in my kidneys that throbbed clear through to my testicles. I was pretty damned mad. "First of all—why?"

"Do you mind if I sit down?" Mandelker went around behind my desk and sat. The son of a bitch was playing movie mogul in my office, and there wasn't much I could do about it without sounding like a spoiled child saying "That's *my* chair!" When he had made himself comfortable he put both hands on the desk in front of him, the cigarette sticking straight up from between his fingers and smoldering like a Comanche signal fire. "You're not unaware of the troubles I've had in the past two years," he said. "It was all an unfortunate misunderstanding, but it left me with a reputation that is, to say the least, suspect."

I nodded. I was with him so far.

"I've committed many indiscretions in my lifetime—as have you—and your friend here—and everyone else. Personal, sexual, financial—we all do things we wouldn't want in the papers, especially those of us in positions of power and wealth." How unselfconsciously he was able to say things like that! "Indiscretions seem to come with the territory in the film business, and because that business holds such a fascination for so many people, we seem to live in more of a goldfish bowl than, say, the insurance executive who's pronging the girl from the typing pool or the stockbroker who juggles figures around so that a few dollars from the client's account goes into his own pocket, or a butcher whose thumb adds eighty cents to the cost of a standing rib roast."

"Sure we do," I said. "Just on a much bigger scale."

He took a last puff on the cigarette and said, "Have it your way, Saxon. At any rate, I got caught, as has been amply documented in every newspaper in the world, and I lost my job as a studio head. But I wound up with an independent production deal that makes me twice the money running a studio ever did. I don't have the immediate power I once did, but I still have a lot, because when you run a major studio in this town you get to know where a lot of the bodies are buried. You have a great deal of information available to you. For instance, Saxon, your first job in this town was playing a helicopter pilot on 'M*A*S*H' in 1975. Your first feature film was a dreary little Western called *The Silent Gun,* a year later. Your agent is Bernie Silverman, your commercial agent is Henry Hiscock, and you've never made more than forty thousand dollars a year as an actor, and that was only one good year. You opened this quaint little business about five years ago, you've done jobs for several people in the business, including Mark Evering and Ron Raskov, and until about eight weeks ago you were living with a travel agent named Leila White, who moved out on you and is now dating an investment counselor in Malibu, name of Thurlow. You're originally from Chicago, the North Side, you are a lapsed Roman Catholic, you served in the army during the Asian unpleasantness but the only action you saw was in the Signal Corps at Fort Gordon, Georgia. You are a very good cook, only not as good as you think you are, and you drink expensive single-malt Scotch—Laphroaig, I believe."

I was stunned almost speechless as I looked at him sitting behind my desk. He knew my entire life, probably the brand of toothpaste I used, and two days before he'd never even heard of me. He had his resources, and I wondered idly how much my dossier had cost him. I also conjectured on how frightened he must have been to have gone to all that trouble, and when I realized he was running a little scared it helped me to get my bearings back somewhat. "What impresses me most," I was finally able to say, "is that you committed all that crap to memory."

He smiled an inscrutable, almost faraway smile. "I remember the first dollar I ever earned and the first woman I ever laid, and most of both since then, too. I also remember who my friends are—and who they are not."

George began to stir on the floor. He wasn't exactly waking up, but he was beginning to twitch a little, and made funny noises that were someplace between speech and whimpering. Ray gave me a questioning look and I nodded, and he leaned down and rapped his knuckles smartly against George's temple, and George stopped twitching and making noises.

"No need to take it out on poor George," Mandelker said.

"We're going to start taking it out on poor Sherwin if we don't start getting some answers pretty soon."

He fixed me with a steely glare. "I can see to it you never work in this town again."

It made me laugh. "That kind of shit went out when Zanuck and Harry Cohn packed it up. Besides, if I don't work Jeff Quinn will support me. Now, I'm waiting."

Mandelker looked over at Ray. He was a powerful and ruthless man, but this look told me he was a physical coward, and that gave me the upper hand because I had Ray and Mandelker didn't seem to have George, at least for a while. The tremor in Mandelker's voice betrayed the image of icy repose he was trying to sell us. "Very well. My reputation seems to have become rather shady since the messiness at Mercury Pictures. Not that it isn't deserved, but . . ." He shrugged a kind of boys-will-be-boys shrug that didn't work. "Since then a lot of people—con men and shakedowners and would-be blackmailers have come after me, thinking they have a pretty easy mark. They keep coming around and taking their sleazy little shots."

"And you pay them off?"

"Never. After coming out of the Mercury thing there's nothing more anyone can do to me. I'm almost inviolate. If the world finds out I've been stealing hubcaps or cheating on my income tax or sodomizing small children, they'll say, 'Oh, well; it's Mandelker, what do you expect?' But I keep George and his friend Milo around just in case—and to discourage similar attempts, such as yours."

"I've told you I'm not trying to shake you down."

"You're certainly being enough of a nuisance, then. You come to me in a restaurant with half the industry looking on, and you tell me you have some mysterious information about Buck Weldon's book and that I won't like it if I read it. I have read it, matter of fact."

"I know you have."

That took him back a giant step but he went gamely on. "I assumed you thought you had hold of some really hot stuff that I'd pay handsomely to have suppressed. So I sent George after you to discourage you and those who might try after you. When he came back and told me how well you handled yourself, I decided I'd best find out with whom I was dealing. That's why I compiled your little dossier. It was impressive, but not so much so that I didn't think George shouldn't pay you another visit, perhaps when you weren't quite so well prepared, and I instructed him to call me when the situation was in hand so we could talk face to face and privately."

"Why? Why talk? Why not just have him give me a beating and to hell with it?"

"Especially after the unfortunate death of Miss Gardner, which I understand the police are treating as murder, I was anxious not to be publicly involved with Buck Weldon in any way, especially through the offices of a cheap little chiseler like you."

I was getting annoyed. I turned to Ray, who had no idea what the hell was going on but was just going along with the program, and I said, "Mess him up some, Ray."

Ray took two steps forward and Mandelker's tune changed. "Just a moment, Saxon—I'm ready to make a deal."

Ray grinned at me. He knew I had no intention of letting him hurt Mandelker. That's not the way either one of us operates. I guess I just wanted to chip some of the snotty-ass façade off Mandelker, to see whether that glacial exterior covered up something squishy soft, and now I had found out, the game was over. Ray went back to standing over George, and I leaned over Mandelker's, or rather my desk, and said, "Well?"

He relaxed a bit and sat back in the chair. "I suppose I could keep sending George and Milo until they found you unarmed and unattended, but that would be tedious and serve no real purpose. So let's see if we can work out some sort of rapprochement here. You tell me what you *think* you have, and then I'll tell you what it's worth to have you keep it to yourself, and I can write you out a check right now. I assure you I'll be generous. I can afford to be."

"First of all," I said, "I wouldn't accept a check from you. I know about your checks." Oh, that felt good! "But the fact is, I've got nothing to sell. I've told you before I don't want your goddamned money!" Easy to say. With a bank balance as anemic as mine, it depressed me that I was such a straight shooter, but it sure pays off, little pals out there in Radioland, when you look in the mirror in the morning and a real person looks back at you and not the face of a whore.

"What *do* you want, then?" Mandelker asked.

110

"I've got what I want. I wanted to find out if you were trying to kill Buck Weldon."

He jumped in the chair and lost some more color.

"But," I continued, "I'm satisfied you're not."

He breathed deep. "How?"

"Murder isn't your thing, Mr. Mandelker. If you didn't want Buck to write about you, you'd send George and Milo after him— and he'd beat the crap out of them, by the way, you really ought to get yourself some better muscle—and then if that didn't work you'd try to buy him. And you'd figure anything you can't buy or intimidate isn't worth the effort and you'd go away. Right?"

"Close enough," Mandelker said. He was not smiling.

"I've heard you described as a killer at the negotiating table, but I don't think you have the balls for real out-and-out murder."

"You make it sound as though not having the capacity for murder is something to be ashamed of," he said.

"And you make it sound as though embezzlement and intimidation and stealing hubcaps is something to be proud of. I'm not sure which is worse."

George started groaning and stirring around again, and in answer to Ray's questioning look I held up a warning hand. To Mandelker I said, "One more thing. You told me I'd never work in this town again. Maybe, maybe not. I don't work that much now. But if I ever hear so much as a whisper—an innuendo, even—that I lost an acting job because of a thumbs-down or a blacklist that started with you—I'm going to have Ray here take George and Milo for a walk and I'm going to come after you myself. Now take your three-picture deal and your bum checks and your gorilla and your ego and get your fat ass out of my chair!"

Mandelker rose up from behind my desk, and his eyes were like agates and there was a white line around his lips. I wondered if he were going to have a stroke, and if he did how long it would take me to get to the telephone and call for help. He said, "You're an unreasonable man, Mr. Saxon. It's no wonder you're so small-time."

Ray hauled George to his feet. George stood there rubbing his eyes with his fist like the little kid in the "Time to re-tire" ad, and Mandelker took his arm and led him out like a pet elephant. It was only then I began to appreciate how much I hurt in the places where George had hit and kicked me.

"You want to fill me in?" Ray Tucek said.

"Not before I pour the drinks."

Ray Tucek belted his liquor down neat in one gulp, and I was grateful the brand of Scotch I kept at the office was not the expensive stuff. He was an agreeable drinking companion nevertheless, and when we had polished off two drinks apiece, he in his violent fashion and I in my slow, savoring sips, I remembered something and said, "Ray, have I thanked you for saving me from a beating?"

"No," he said, "but then you always did have the manners of a renegade Apache. Anyway, no big deal. Guys that size usually don't know how to handle themselves. They figure their size alone is going to keep them out of more fights than it gets them into. Now tell me—how does Mandelker fit in here?"

I told him, and when I'd finished Ray had another drink and said, "I guess we'll both be on the shit list now."

"Just the opposite, I'd think. Mandelker gets nervous when he's *mano a mano*. He'll take on the board of directors or the entire Screen Actors Guild without batting an eye, but you threaten to punch him in that eye and he turns into a wuss. I think my threat will help us get jobs. If he hears I haven't had a part in a month he's going to start to sweat and do something about it. Jesus, I wish I'd have thought of this ten years ago—I'd be a star!"

"You believe him about Weldon?"

"I don't know. Sounded logical. Like I said, he just isn't the type."

"So we eliminate Mandelker from our list of suspects?"

"You talk like Agatha Christie sometimes, Ray. No, we don't eliminate him yet. Which reminds me, why aren't you at Weldon's watching the store?"

"Because his incredible-looking daughter came out to my car and told me she was going to be home all evening and that I might as well get some sleep. Okay?"

"Sure," I said, visions of said daughter and the way she looked in my bedroom when I peeled her out of that peach-colored batwing outfit dancing in my head the way no sugarplum ever had, and I was cognizant of that big empty place inside me, hollow and dark, that characterized the walking-around condition of the lonely. I shook it off. "Let me give you some money as long as you're here."

"If you got it, fine," Ray said. "If not, you can owe me. I know you're good for it."

I took out my desk-size checkbook. "You sure?"

He grinned. "You saw what I did to George."

"That's what I like about you, Ray, you've such a good head for business." I wrote out a check for one week's bodyguarding, tore it from the ledger and handed it to him. "You'll be back on the job in the morning?"

"Crack of sparrows," Ray said. "It's a good thing we're so anxious for Buck Weldon to stay alive, because he sure as hell isn't worrying about it."

"What do you mean?"

Ray sat forward on the sofa, elbows on hammy thighs, and made a vague gesture with his hands like molding a large lump of clay into a bigger-than-life-size bust. "He just doesn't act like a guy whose life has been threatened. He goes to Ralph's market, he goes to the cleaners, he comes out and potchkeys around the front yard with some peppermint plants he's got working out there—all like nothing's been happening."

"No furtive looks around to see if anyone's following?"

"Not at all. I've been changing cars and changing looks every day. I've done the well-to-do Valley executive, the repairman, the aging hippie—but he doesn't seem to give a shit whether he's being shadowed or not. If he did make me, he'd have no way of knowing if I was there to guard him or snuff him, but he just doesn't look around."

I chewed on a rough spot inside my lower lip. "What do you make of all that, Ray?"

He waved my check. "Bodyguarding's one price, psychiatric

evaluation's another. But I'd say he acts like a man who doesn't care one way or the other."

I stayed after Ray left, my gut aching, my head throbbing, and a sharp knife pain shooting through my kidneys that I couldn't help thinking Mandelker and George had not properly paid for. But there wasn't much to do about that now except quietly drink until the aches didn't matter any more, and I really didn't want to do that either, because after too much liquor thinking became non-productive, and I needed to think. I used my final swallow of whisky to knock down three Panadols and hoped that the pain would go away.

Buck had almost been run off the road, Marsh Zeidler had been shot at, Shelley had snorted the deadly poisoned cocaine meant for Buck, and all that pointed to the work of an amateur. Sometimes they were infinitely more dangerous because of their unpredictability. Deke James had reason enough to hate Buck, and it wasn't the type of hatred that would go away because the fires would get refueled every time Deke lifted his hand to scratch his nose. But he'd had a year and a half to take his best shot and hadn't done so. Valerie sponged off Buck and used him and disrespected him, but he was her meal ticket. Bo Kullander lionized and overanalyzed him, but in a totally detached way. Elliot Knaepple sold him like a prime cut of beef and cared only for his ten percent, but he cared much for that. Sherwin Mandelker really feared him, perhaps too much to kill him. Jeremy Radisson lived in splendor from the money Buck made him and had tried to cheat him out of more, and their long-standing symbiotic relationship was being threatened. What a hatful of suspects!

And then Tori—Tori the bruised and the beautiful, Tori of my reveries, who had touched me once and then retreated back into her walled garden of loneliness—could Tori want her father dead? I had to assume not, for two reasons. The first was that it was she who had hired me to protect him and find his would-be assassin. The second was that I could not have borne it if she were the one; I would have buckled like a skyscraper made of nubby plywood. No, it had to not be Tori. Please, God.

The cleaning crew broke harshly into my ruminations, a wiry

Chicano and his plump, pretty wife accompanied in their night rounds by their two small children, a girl and a boy of just under school age, with huge brown serious eyes that belied the laughter bubbling just behind the corners of their pretty baby mouths. While their parents worked quickly and efficiently, the boy and girl sat on the couch in my private office with their little legs sticking straight out in front of them, on their best behavior. The girl carried a baby doll wrapped in swaddling clothes and the boy was equipped with a comic book and a couple of rubbery plastic doll figures of fantastic space monsters with swiveling arms and heads and legs. I wished I'd had some candy to give them, but I gave them what I did have—a smile. Then I got out of the way of their hard-working guardians.

"Make sure you vacuum," I told the man as I left.

It was drizzling when I got downstairs, that heavy mist that soaks you before you know it's there. The drizzle was the seeming capper to a pretty lousy day all around, but it wasn't until I bent to unlock my car door that I realized the Fates had not finished fucking with me on this particular day. It could have been anything hard and metallic that was poked into the small of my back, very near my aching kidney, but the little click I heard told me it was indeed a gun. I straightened up slowly and raised my hands to shoulder level, my car keys still dangling from my fingers. "Move!" was the guttural bark in my ear, and the gun nudged me in the desired direction. I thought of my own gun nestled beneath the driver's seat of my car, close enough to touch but not close enough to avoid getting shot going for it. I heaved a sigh as I walked. I couldn't very well go around with a pistol in my hand all the time, and anything less seemed to be inadequate these days.

The thing in my back guided me toward a four-door Sedan de Ville parked near the back of the lot. When we reached it the voice said, "Get in back. Slide all the way over." The voice was beginning to sound familiar but I couldn't quite place it. I didn't have to, though, because when I obeyed orders and slid across to the Caddy's far side, Deke James crawled in after me, his .22-caliber pistol preceding him by an arm's length. It wasn't much gun—but across the seat of a Sedan de Ville he didn't need much more than that. The door shut, the dome light went out, and I settled back against the upholstered softness of the seat and waited. This was his party, after all, because he had the gun.

Tori Weldon's former husband just looked at me, his weapon pointed in the general vicinity of my navel. I couldn't see the expression on his face, but I judged it was probably not friendly. This seemed to be excessive retaliation for a small punch in the ribs, but then I reasoned there might be a host of other things he wanted to talk about enough to make the long haul from Mimosa Beach in the rain. Finally he said, "No sucker punches this time. I could fuck up your face real bad."

"Go ahead," I said a lot more unconcerned than I felt. "I'll tell the papers it was an automobile accident on the Pacific Coast Highway."

I heard him breathing through his nose, whistling slightly. I said, "How did you find me?"

"First I called the Hearst papers," he said, "and they'd never heard of anyone named Saxon. That made me nervous. Then when I read about Shelley Gardner in the paper I got even more nervous. So I hired a private detective."

I started to laugh. Between Deke's own private snoop and Sherwin Mandelker's investigative team I seemed to be very popular on the gumshoe circuit in the last few days. I was only a trifle bitter that neither of those jobs had come through my agency, but I guess that was a bit much to ask.

"Like you," Deke said. "A cheap transom-peeper, just like you. You weren't worth the money I paid."

"You make me feel like a camera made in Taiwan. Well, here I am, Deke. Say your piece. Or shoot me. Or whatever you're going to do. It's been a hard day."

"I want to know why you came to my home to bother me."

"I'm a fan. Pure celebrity worship."

"Try again, and make it good this time or I'll smash your face."

"Oh, you've come up in the world from beating up women?" The gun wavered. "I know all about your 'accident' last year, Deke. And I know why, too."

"Buck Weldon—that miserable fucking bastard!" he said. He didn't have Joe DiMattia's flair for profanity. "It was none of his business!" he said like a small boy. He might have been saying

116

"beeswax" instead. Then he said, "So what, Saxon—I've never done anything to you."

I had to think on that. He hadn't—and what he'd done to Tori was long before I ever knew of her existence. What I really wanted to know now, personal feelings about him aside for the moment, was whether he was trying to do anything to Buck Weldon. I told him so. I said, "Since three attempts have been made on his life, I'm trying to find all the people who might have reasons for wanting him to die. You're right up there on the Hate Parade."

He wasn't even pointing the gun at me any more. He was lost in a bubbling stockpot of resentment. "A whole career into the shitter," he murmured, his eyes fixed firmly on some point inside his own skull. "Walking around like a ninety-year-old man for the rest of my life—and the pain in my knuckles when the weather gets damp, like now—I damn near want to cry sometimes."

I was afraid he would suit the action to the word. I didn't want Deke James to cry. I didn't want to feel sorry for him. He had fucked the woman I loved and then he had punched and tormented her, and he was only getting what he deserved, I figured, and yet here he was, in the backseat of his expensive car with a gun clutched in his broken fingers, and he was ready to weep over his losses—loss of glory, loss of income, loss of Tori. Maybe it had never occurred to him before what a total loser he was—and for an athlete that's a gut shot. At least he'd never had to admit it to anyone before—thereby admitting it to himself.

"Did you try to shoot him, Deke? Or spike his blow?"

"Only because I never thought of it." He sounded weary, now. The gun was just lying in his lap. "Who hired you anyway?" he said.

"Sorry, that's confidential."

"Never mind, I know. She sic you on me?"

"Nobody sicced me on anybody. I've talked to a lot of people who know Buck—you're just one."

"I haven't even seen him since—for a year or more."

"I couldn't know that till I asked."

"You ask too much."

"That's how you learn."

"Sometimes you learn more than you ought to."

My personal dislike for him overwhelmed my professional aplomb for a moment and I said, "You mean because I learned about your so-called car crash? That a sixty-year-old man beat you up and broke your hands? Is that what you mean?"

Someone yanked on the string attached to the back of his neck because his body jerked convulsively, and then the gun came up a few inches again, as though he'd forgotten he had it and then suddenly remembered. His voice was tight. "Shut up about that," he said. "You'd better shut up about that."

"Why? Afraid your little beach bunnies might hear about it and cut off your nookie?"

The gun wavered again. "God damn you, Saxon."

"See, Deke, I know all about you. I know you've got a great reason for wanting Buck Weldon dead."

"Sure I got a reason!" Deke cried out. "These!" I was getting tired of him holding his hands up as a supplicant for the world's pity. "But I didn't try to kill him. The fucker! I hope whoever it is gets lucky next time."

"Deke," I said, "you're the original dickless wonder. People who beat up women to prove how tough they are rank right up there on the scale with guys who mug old ladies or wave their peepees at kids in a schoolyard. I think Buck was too easy on you—I would have broken your legs, too." That was pretty chancy to say to a man with a gun, but I thought I had my customer figured out right. I unlocked the door on my side of the car and opened it a little, enough to hear the rain hissing on the asphalt. "I'm leaving now, Deke. You can use that gun if you want to—but you better not miss, because if you do I'm going to take it away from you and put it up your ass."

The rain felt good on my face, cold and bracing, and I took my time walking from Deke's car to my own little rag-top, not really worrying about a bullet in the back, because I was learning that cowards and bullies like Deke James and Sherwin Mandelker didn't like threats of violence against themselves. It scared them. I'd have to remember that if it came up again, and I was sure it would, because the world is full of bullies and cowards.

*   *   *

To the west, in my own little fortress in the Palisades, my answering machine was blinking the glad tidings that someone had called, and after I stripped down to my shorts and fixed myself a mushroom-and-cheese omelette with fresh basil and serrano chiles washed down with a John Courage beer, I listened to the playback. Two hang-ups, a reminder from my dentist that I was due for a cleaning, a message from a jazz singer friend of mine that he'd be appearing for two weeks at a bar in Glendale, a call from Ray obviously placed before he'd seen me at the office, and a rather frantic message from Marshall Zeidler. I knew Marsh could get frantic when the tide went out, so I decided to call Tori Weldon first.

Her hello was warm and muzzy from sleep, and I remembered she'd told Ray she was turning in early. I tried to imagine her there alone in her bed, her hair tousled, probably wearing an oversized T-shirt in lieu of pajamas, and I wanted to be with her, beside her, so much that it hurt right under my breastbone. I tried creative visualization to transport me there to her, but it didn't work.

"I'm sorry to wake you," I said, "but I need to talk to you."

"I told you I can't handle it right now," she began, but I cut her off with my secondary reason for calling.

"It's about the key to Shelley's apartment. Did you get it?"

There was a long pause, and I hoped perhaps she was a little miffed that I hadn't called her for personal reasons. Then, "Yes, I have it."

"Good. Can you meet me there tomorrow at ten?"

"Can't you come out here and pick it up?"

"Sure," I said, "and when your father wants to know what I'm doing there we'll just explain to him how I want to look through his dead girlfriend's things. I'm sure he'll be fine about it."

I heard her lighting one of her evil brown cigarettes. "All right," she said, "ten o'clock." I didn't say anything. "Look, I don't mean to be—I'm just very frightened."

"For your father?"

"Yes," she said with an upward inflection. "And of you."

"I'll file the points off my fangs and see you at ten," I said. "And since it's business I'll try not to get weak in the knees when I see you."

I hung up. A complex lady was Tori Weldon, and I knew somehow that if I got involved with her there would be dues to be paid. But she was worth it.

I dialed the Zeidlers' home number and Jo answered. "This phone call will cost you overtime," she said, "I'm off duty. How was Palm Springs?"

"Like you'd think it would be the week before Christmas in the rain," I said. "And never mind the overtime. I'm returning Marshall's call."

"Good," she said, "he's been very mysterious all evening. Maybe you can figure it out."

When Marsh took the phone I could hear him breathing in short, agitated little gulps. I said, "Marsh, are you all right?"

"Yeah, I'm fine. Listen, I've figured out the Buck Weldon case."

I felt the tension running out of my neck and shoulders. This was going to be good. I cradled the phone against the side of my head and moved to the refrigerator for another John Courage. The cupboard was bare, damn it. I poured myself a neat Laphroaig, which is really what I'd wanted in the first place. "How'd you do that, Marsh?"

"Look," Marsh said in a very logical, almost pedantic tone. I could see him frowning earnestly, pushing his glasses back up over his nose with his index finger. "You've read all Buck Weldon's books, or most of them, and the message comes across loud and clear. He has a natural enemy, an implacable enemy, one that would be a lot better off if he stopped writing for good."

"Oh?" I said. "Who's that?"

There was a beat taken for dramatic effect, than almost triumphantly he said, "Organized crime. The Mafia!"

I thanked Marsh for his splendid suggestion and told him I'd give it some thought. After I hung up, I did—about two seconds' worth of conjecture that organized crime would try to kill a mystery novelist of Buck's stature for lousing up their public image. Then I went into the bathroom. In addition to the dust of the road to and from the desert, and the dust of my office carpet, there was a thin sheen of emotional and psychological dirt that had been deposited on me by Jeremy Radisson and Sherwin Mandelker and George the Enforcer and Deke James, and I wanted to wash it off.

The hot shower was only the first step.

○ 10 ○

Morning comes early when you aren't working at a nine-to-five job and are used to getting up whenever you feel like it, and the blast of heavy-metal rock from the clock radio was just what I needed to get me out of bed and across the room to turn it off. I always figured that if I set my wake-up alarm to good music, the temptation to lie in bed and listen to it would be too great, but the clankings and wailings of Ozzy Osbourne offered no such seductiveness. I peered out my window and noted with pleasure that we were having a rare day of December sunshine, and that made the trip out to Encino seem more agreeable. Besides, the thought of seeing Tori again was making something wonderful and foreign flutter around in my chest, battering its tiny determined wings against my ribs.

She had parked on the street in front of Shelley Gardner's apartment building, standing by the car with the sunlight doing remarkable things to her hair. She wore a black jacket over a green silk blouse and black pants, and I marveled at the way everything she wore seemed to top the outfit before. If she was as glad to see me as I to see her, she managed to camouflage that fact very nicely. "I really feel funny about this," she said as she handed me a small silver key. "It's ghoulish."

"It's necessary," I said, "and you look gorgeous."

She seemed uncomfortable with the familiarity and she lowered her eyes. I decided to back off on the personal stuff for a while. Some day Tori and I were going to have a long talk about Us—but now was not the time.

Shelley's apartment was a nighttime place, furnished for a nighttime person. In the daylight it looked mournful, like an aging harlot whose makeup job, designed for the soft light of a cocktail lounge, shows its seams in the sunshine. There was a half-empty pack of cigarettes on the coffee table, and in the kitchen sink the remnants of a long-ago sandwich stood next to a wineglass with lipstick on the rim. Both plate and glass had been rinsed but not washed. There was also a filter tip with the same shade of lipstick in a small ashtray stolen from a Las Vegas hotel on the drainboard. It was very sad, and both of us felt the sadness, even though Tori hadn't particularly liked Shelley Gardner and I'd only met her once. There were vibrations in this room, palpable memories that belonged to someone else but still made me want to shudder.

"Exactly what are we looking for?" Tori said.

"I don't know. Where's the bedroom?"

"I don't know, either. I've never been here before."

There was just one hallway leading off the living room, and we entered it and found the bedroom with no trouble. It was white like the rest of the apartment, with a king-size bed under a satin coverlet and a white satin headboard to go with it. The bed had been made but there was an indentation as though someone had sat down on the spread. I wondered if any two ass-prints were alike. Another open pack of cigarettes was on the nightstand, along with a white telephone and white tooled-leather address book. I sat on the bed and flipped through the book, but there were no surprises. Buck's number was there, and Valerie's, and a woman named Doris Willett on the W page. I looked in vain for numbers for Jeremy Radisson, Elliot Knaepple or Deke James, and wasn't sure what it might have meant had I found them there. I wandered over to the dresser and found nothing of import on its surface, just a rather messy makeup kit and the strong perfume that Shelley had overused and whose scent seemed to cling to the carpets and walls. There were several shades of lip gloss but only one of them showed much sign of use. I went through the drawers very quickly, finding blouses and folded sweaters and lingerie. In the back of one of the drawers was a photograph album, and I took it out and looked through it. There were a lot of pictures of Buck Weldon on its pages—Buck barbecuing steaks, Buck at his typewriter looking annoyed at the intrusion of the flashbulb, Buck up in the redwoods, Buck at the ocean, and several scenes of Buck and Shelley together, smiling in those unnatural poses couples adopt when they've asked a stranger to take a snapshot of them at Disneyland. Near the back of the album, not mounted on the paper but simply stuck in between the pages, was a snap of an elderly couple standing in front of a white midwestern-style clapboard house. If one looked closely, the woman bore more than a passing resemblance to Shelley. Obviously they were her parents back home in wherever-it-was in the Midwest, and I wondered if they still lived, if they were grieving over their daughter's senseless and brutal death, and whether they had ever grieved over her life as Buck Weldon's doxy. I knew little of Shelley's background. I'd assumed she was an actress or showgirl of some sort before taking up with Buck, but there were no theatrical pictures of any kind, nor any pictures of the younger Shelley, the high school grad Shelley, the prom Shelley, the First Communion Shelley. Except for the browning photo of her parents, Shelley might have sprung full-blown to become Buck's lover.

Tori was watching me closely and, I hope, with some fascination. "Make yourself useful, darling," I said. "Go look through the closet."

"What am I looking for?"

"Anything that doesn't belong in a closet. An elephant, a 'fifty-five Chevy, anything. I'll check the chest of drawers over here."

More clothes. An inlaid Chinese box with some inexpensive costume jewelry. If Buck had bought her any of the real thing she'd stashed it somewhere safe, because the most expensive item in the box, a diamond cocktail ring, couldn't have cost more than two hundred dollars. There was a Minolta thirty-five-millimeter camera in an imitation leather case in the drawers, and back behind some folded slacks was a bong, the type of smoking device that could be purchased in any head shop, and a Ziploc sandwich bag full of what, on closer examination, turned out to be marijuana. There was less than an ounce there, and given the proclivities of most of Los Angeles, its presence in Shelley's drawer was not terribly unusual. I stuck the bag into my jacket pocket and kept looking.

"Anything?" I said to Tori.

She shook her head. "Two tennis rackets, an overnight case, about a million pairs of shoes, a picnic ice chest—just the normal stuff."

I knelt to look under the bed, and my efforts were rewarded

with some dust bunnies, a pair of high-heeled bedroom slippers, fourteen cents, and a stub from the movie theatre in the Galleria. Tori said, "This is making me very uncomfortable. Can't we get out of here?"

"In good time," I said. "After we check the kitchen again."

The kitchen drawers yielded silverware, utensils, a whole drawerful of cents-off coupons clipped from the Sunday papers, and a three-to-a-page checkbook with an imitation snakeskin cover—in white. I took it to the dining room table, switching on the overhead chandelier and turning the dimmer up to high. I saw check stubs whose dates started about seven months earlier, in May. Rent checks, Visa checks, checks to Bullock's and Saks, and a lot of checks to Gelman's Supermarket. Obviously Shelley had been like most of us and used her local grocer as a bank. And then, beginning in August, I found something that interested me. There were check stubs dated August 8, September 13, October 19, November 19, and December 12, just two days before Shelley's death. The stubs were not totally filled out. They bore only the date, the amount—$750 each time—and the cryptic notation "Val."

I didn't say anything to Tori but I copied down the check information in my notebook. Tori, in the meantime, had opened another drawer and found a stack of unpaid bills, including a telephone bill on which I almost pounced. It was for the preceding month, but there were two calls to Valerie Weldon's number in Westwood, one on the fifteenth of November and one on the eighteenth—the day before the date of Shelley's November check to Val. I jotted all the information down, including the time of day—both calls had been in the morning. Then I put the checkbook and the bills back where they belonged.

"I don't know what you hoped to prove by all this," Tori said.

"Nothing, just being thorough. Isn't that what you're paying me for?"

We left the apartment pretty much the way we had found it, and were walking past the pool toward the front entrance where we both had parked our cars. I put my arm around her shoulders, and she stiffened slightly.

"I won't hurt you," I said.

"I'm not afraid of you."

"Yes you are, Tori. You're afraid that I might love you and then you'd have to love me back, and that scares the hell out of you. I don't know why. Two people can love each other."

"Prove it!" she said. There was cynicism behind those bruised eyes.

"I'd like to, but you won't give me a chance."

We got to the cars and she said, "I haven't meant to be cold these past few days. It's just that this thing is so horrible—I can't think about anything except my own problems." And she turned and smiled at me and turned my knees to raspberry Jell-O, and at the same time I had a sick feeling in my heart because those check stubs had told me something I wished they hadn't, and I was afraid that I was going to have to hurt Tori very badly after all.

I reached out and put my hand on the back of her hair and said, "It's okay. We can talk when this is over." She unlocked her car door and started to get in, and then she straightened up and kissed me on the mouth, one of those kisses that promises so much, and then she was gone, down the street in the hard-edged sunshine, and I didn't know whether to laugh or cry. I felt like crying but was a bit too self-conscious to do so on a busy street in Encino. I didn't do either one, but flipped open the top of my car to take advantage of the rare good weather. On the trip down the freeway to Westwood the cool air felt good against my face and in my hair.

Valerie Weldon was out when I arrived at her apartment building on Ohio Avenue, so I sat down by the small swimming pool and read the newspaper I'd picked up from my doorstep that morning but had not taken the time to read. There wasn't much on the sports page except Super Bowl hype; "Dear Abby" was a repeat of a column she'd written ten years ago about loving your parents while they're still alive; a lot of the front section stories were about Third World politicians. It was evidently what journalists call a "slow news day." So I contented myself browsing through reviews of the blockbuster holiday film releases, none of which, I was sorry to say, I was in.

Finally, when I'd been reduced to reading "Rex Morgan, M.D.," on the comics page, Valerie came through the gate. She was wearing form-hugging tights and a leotard and a big bulky cowl-neck sweater of the type worn by fifties beatniks in Greenwich Village.

She carried a bag of groceries, and she looked every bit as luscious as the first time I'd met her. I disliked her every bit as much, too.

"Well, I never expected to find you on my doorstep," she said. "But I love pleasant surprises. You couldn't have picked a better time."

"Why's that?"

"Abdul hasn't been around for a few days and I'm horny as hell."

"This isn't a social call, Val. We need to talk."

"Talk, talk, talk," she groused, handing me the groceries to carry, "doesn't anybody ever fuck any more?" She led me through the lobby to the elevator and up to her apartment. She unlocked the door and stood aside so I could go in ahead of her. "Welcome to Castle Dracula," she said.

I put the groceries down on the counter between the living and dining areas as she indicated, and she brushed past me to the refrigerator. The brush was all with her breasts, as seductive as hell, and I realized once more what a healthy young animal Valerie Weldon was. She opened the refrigerator door and said, "Is it too early in the day for a drink?"

"I told you, Valerie, I'm here to talk seriously."

She peered at me over the door. "Your loss, Saxon, I'd turn you every way but loose." She rummaged in the crisper drawer. "How about a joint, then, to ease the tension?" She brought out a plastic bag full of weed, similar to the one I now had in my pocket that had belonged to Shelley. "Stays fresher when you keep it in the fridge."

I went over and took the bag of grass away from her and put it on the countertop. "You've got your whole life to get stoned," I said, "but you'd better be straight right now if you know what's good for you."

"Hey!" she said, making a grab for the bag and banging up against me in the process. Valerie was the one for whom the phrase "too close for comfort" was coined. I stepped back away from her. "You've got your fucking nerve walking in here—"

"Val—"

"I don't need this shit!"

"Sit down, Val."

"Who do you think—?"

"I'm the guy who's either going to talk to you or talk to the police."

That seemed to quiet her down some, draining the color from those cheeks still larded with baby fat. Her eyes were bright and glittery, her heavy breasts rose and fell with each breath. She didn't know whether she should stay defiant or break down and be a little girl, so I led her into the living room before she could make a decision. Since I hadn't allowed her a drink or a joint, she lit a cigarette with a rather childish pout.

"A shame what happened to Shelley Gardner," I said carefully. She was smoking furiously. "Tough break."

"Yeah. Tough break for Dad."

"It just might be a tough break for you, Val."

"Why?"

"Because you were the one who's been supplying your father and Shelley with cocaine all along—and you were the one who delivered the batch that killed her."

The hand holding the cigarette trembled. "You can't prove that," she said with a mouthful of smoke that made her cough.

"I can give the police enough evidence to make it really uncomfortable for you," I said, and I told her about the check stubs and the phone calls.

"I didn't kill Shelley, for God's sake."

"Maybe not. And maybe the cops won't think so either, I don't know. But dealing drugs isn't like a ticket for overtime parking at a meter."

"Dealing? Now, wait a minute, Saxon, I'm not into dealing. Nobody can say—"

"Valerie!" I took her by the arms hard enough that when I finally took my hands away my finger marks were livid on her skin. "Shelley Gardner died from bad cocaine, cocaine that you got for her. Now if you didn't kill her, you'd better start talking pretty damned fast, or I'll be at police headquarters in ten minutes and you can talk to them."

She slumped down on the sofa like a broken doll four days after Christmas, her arms listlessly at her sides and her chin on her chest and her legs splayed out in front of her.

"It was last spring," she said. "Shelley's coke connection got busted and she didn't know where to go. She called me and asked if I knew where she could score once in a while, and I told her I'd help her out, that's all. About once a month I'd get a call from her and I'd get her whatever she needed. I'd bring the stuff out there to the house when I came to dinner, and she'd give me a check for it. That's all I know."

"Did you know your father was using, too?"

"Nobody ever told me. But nobody had to. Yeah, I guess I knew. So what?"

"So what!!"

"I do blow sometimes and it never hurt me any. So I didn't think much about it."

"Seven fifty a pop is a lot of blow."

"Well," she said, "there was a commission."

I wondered if the distaste I felt for her showed on my face, and then I didn't care if it did or not. Apparently it did, because she hastened to say, "Listen, I put my ass on the line every time I drove over the pass with that stuff in my car!"

I tried patience. "Okay, Val, now think back. Shelley called you on the ninth or tenth of December and said she was needy. On the twelfth you delivered it to her and she wrote you a check for it. On the fourteenth she was dead. Now I want to know everything that happened between the time she called you and the time you made delivery."

"Nothing happened. She called me—I don't remember which day. I said okay. So I told Abdul and he brought the stuff home on the eleventh. I delivered it on the twelfth and put the check in the bank. That's all I know."

Abdul! Why wasn't anything ever easy? I said, "You mean Abdul is the one who gets the coke for you?"

"Yeah," she said. "He told me he had a good supplier and that he'd take care of it."

"Who was his supplier?"

"How do I know?"

"Someplace at school?"

"I don't know."

"Not Snuffy's?"

"Snuffy's is just a place where heads hang out. You can't really

128

score anything over there, there's too much heat hanging around all the time."

"And you don't know who it is at school. Another kid?"

"I don't give a shit where he gets it. Why should I?"

"Where is Abdul now?"

"I don't know."

"Guess."

"I couldn't. He lives on Sepulveda." She gave me the address and I copied it in my book. "Abdul wouldn't kill anybody."

"How would you know?"

"I just know. I don't think we've talked about Buck or Shelley three times in the six months we've been together. He's got more important things to think about."

"I'll bet," I said.

"Jesus, you can be a pain in the ass!"

"Part of my fatal charm. Where should I look for Abdul?"

She shrugged. "Maybe at Snuffy's. Like I told you, he hasn't been around here the past few days."

"Why not?"

She shrugged again, and her face was as sad as a little girl's that had been painted to look like a woman's. "Maybe because it's the wrong time of the month."

The bartender at Snuffy's recognized me right away. "Hey, here comes Mr. Excitement," he said, squinting through the smoke of his cigarette. "Looking for some kicks again, I bet."

"Not this time," I told him. "I'm looking for Abdul Muhammad. Has he been in here?"

"I wouldn't know," the bartender said.

"Was he in here yesterday?"

"I wouldn't know."

I took a twenty-dollar bill from my pocket and held it between my second and third fingers like a cigarette. "You sure?"

He looked at me with contempt and disgust. "Get outa my face! Whaddyou, kiddin' me?"

I leaned forward and slapped him across the nose with the twenty and with my two fingers. It didn't hurt, but it startled him, enough for me to grab his shirt and pull him toward me until his feet were almost off the ground on the other side of the bar. "Listen, scumbag, I'm tired of fucking with you. Now you talk to me or I'll have every narc on the West Side up your ass."

I felt an alligator bite me on the left shoulder, and I turned around to see an enormous, bearded man in a black T-shirt that said EAT PUSSY all over it. His shaggy beard was red-blond and he wore a blue and white railroad bandanna across his forehead. The eyes that glowered at me were the size and color of tarnished dimes, and his breath smelled of Coors beer and Dubble-Bubble gum. His skin was flounder-white, in vivid contrast to his yellow teeth and the dirt-clogged pores around his nose. He pushed his face far too close to mine and said, "You don't come in here and put your hands on Bill like that, mister."

I was somehow quite sorry that the bartender's name was Bill and not Snuffy after all. Oh, well, another one of life's little disappointments. I said to the biker, "Look, somebody's life is in danger—"

"Yours," the Red Beard said.

"I don't want any trouble—"

"Well, you got some. A whole shit-pot full."

I think I have survived as long as I have by knowing my limitations. Although I play a decent jazz piano, I don't sit down to tinkle when Oscar Peterson is in the room. As an actor, I've never attempted to play King Lear, and I've never tried to slug it out with a man the size and disposition of an Alaskan Kodiak bear. So, much as I disliked doing it, I decided to use my edge.

Red Beard released his wolf-trap grip on my shoulder and took a small, clumsy step backward when he felt the muzzle of my .38 poking into his bloated belly, and his mean little eyes got bigger. I motioned him to stand back against the bar so that both he and the bartender, Bill, were facing me. I glanced over my shoulder, but no one else was in Snuffy's. Perhaps I was going to get away with it.

"It's too damn bad," I said, "that some people have to do things the hard way."

There was a long wait, and the bartender said, "You're a damn Gestapo."

I just laughed.

Bill said, "Abdul hasn't been in here for a couple of days."

130

"Isn't that unusual?" I said. "I thought he was here every day."

"Abdul?" Red Beard said. "That big nigger?"

"Yeah, it's unusual," Bill told me, wiping at his nose. "But I'm not his fucking nursemaid."

I took one of my cards out of my pocket and gave it to Bill. "If you see him, have him contact me right away. It's important."

He looked at the card and his shoulders slumped. "Shit—you aren't the heat after all."

"I never said I was, Bill, you did."

I sighed and put the gun back in its holster, after making sure I had stepped far enough away from Red Beard so that I could get it again in a hurry before he was all over me. He was breathing loudly through his mouth, sulking as if I'd just repossessed his Harley. Bill had gone back to wiping down the bar and it was to him I addressed my exit line.

"Now, wouldn't it have been nicer," I said, "to take the twenty bucks?"

The address Valerie had given me for Abdul Muhammad was an apartment building on Sepulveda Boulevard south of National, converted from a single-family dwelling during the great California migration after the Second World War. The pseudo-Spanish stucco walls had been painted a bilious mauve, but the ancient cracks in the driveway had not been repaired since the original construction. The paper shades behind the cheap nylon curtains in the windows made sure that light never penetrated inside, making it as dark as a vampire's lair. Abdul's apartment was in the back, Number 6. From his next-door neighbor I heard the amplified driving beat of Kool and the Gang, but behind Abdul's door there was no sound.

I knocked, waited, then knocked a second time. If Abdul was in there, he wasn't planning on answering my summons. I tried the doorknob without any great expectations; this was not a neighborhood where anyone with a dollop of sense left doors unlocked. When I couldn't gain entry I went to the front of the building, to Number 1, which bore a red and white sign telling me the manager was in residence here. The door was open but the screen door was hooked.

The manager was a woman of indeterminate size and weight. If

I'd had to guess I would have called her age at the late fifties and her weight some four times that. Her eyes were a dull brown, and the corners of her mouth seemed to be inordinately susceptible to the pull of gravity. There were several warts and moles in the folds of her double chin, and her mustache was of the style once sported by George Brent. There was a smell about her of milk that was not quite fresh.

"Is Mr. Muhammad in trouble of some sort?" she said when I had inquired of Abdul's whereabouts.

"No, I just need to talk to him. It's business."

"Well, I don't get too friendly with the tenants," she said, "it's bad policy. Of course he's never here too much. He's got a girlfriend he stays with a lot." She lowered her voice to impart the shameful secret. "A white girl. But that's his affair, it don't bother me none. I'm glad to say I'm not prejudice."

I nodded. "Has he been here this morning?"

"I'm sure I couldn't say. As long as people pay their rent on time and don't make too much noise—of course, some of them nigroes, they play their rock radio awful loud."

I was glad she wasn't prejudice. "When is the last time you saw him?"

"A few days ago, I guess."

"I wonder if I could take a look in his apartment?"

"Oh, no," she said, "that wouldn't be right. It wouldn't be legal, even."

I showed her my license. "I'm an officer of the court," I said. That wasn't true, but I doubt if the manager was up on civil law.

"Even still," she protested.

"It might be very important. A matter of life or death. It'll just take a moment."

She didn't waver. "I'm afraid it's impossible," she said primly, enjoying her role as guardian of the gates. "I mean, I don't know you or anything, even."

I had anticipated her reluctance. I gave her the twenty-dollar bill that Snuffy's bartender had refused. The twenty disappeared into the maw of her housedress pocket. "Well," she said. "Then I'll have to go in with you—just for my tenant's protection."

"I'm not going to steal the family silver," I said.

"Even still."

She disappeared into her apartment for a time, and I stood there waiting in the chilly sunshine while I heard her rummage around inside. Finally she reappeared with a set of keys bound together with a piece of dirty string, and led me back to Number 6 as though she were an offensive lineman blocking for Walter Payton. She certainly had the bulk for it. She tried a few keys in the door until I heard the tumblers click. She opened the door about two inches and then stood aside so I could go in first. Just in case. Her caution was seemingly built-in.

I stepped into the dingy apartment and the smell stung my nose immediately, sickly sweet and acrid at the same time, and I gulped back the sudden wave of nausea that was pushing at the back of my throat. I put my hand out to the side, palm backward, to stop her from coming in any further, but she'd gotten just far enough through the door to see the same thing I saw, and I heard her suck in about three liters of air preparatory to screaming, so I turned around quickly and eased her out onto the walkway before she had a chance.

"Shhh," I said, though she hadn't made a sound yet. "Go on back to your place and call the police."

"Sweet Jesus," she wailed.

"Go on."

"Oh my Sweet Jesus! Nothing like this has ever happened here. I run a clean place—"

"Go!" I snapped. Her thin lips, incongruous amidst the rolls of fat surrounding her face, suddenly clamped tightly together, and one hand seemingly possessed of a mind of its own moved up to pull nervously on her fleshy cheek. She nodded numbly and turned to scurry—as much as she could manage to scurry at her weight—back to the sanctuary of her own little place, praying to Sweet Jesus as she went.

I held my breath and stepped back into the apartment. The furniture was unremarkable, the type one would expect to find in that kind of furnished place, naugahyde and pine and thrift-shop modern. Abdul Muhhamad was lying on his back in front of the sofa. He was wearing a pair of blue jeans, but was shirtless and barefoot. His chocolate skin had a gray undertinge to it, and from that and the smell I figured he'd been dead at least forty-eight hours. If his killer was the same one who had run Buck's car off the road, shot at Marsh Zeidler, and slipped Shelley Gardner some poisoned cocaine, he certainly had eclectic tastes in murder: Abdul was the victim of a broken neck.

By the time the police finished with me it was three o'clock in the afternoon. I'd had a moment of panic because when they had arrived at Abdul's apartment I realized I still had a bag of marijuana in my pocket, but fortunately I wasn't searched. The detective who had talked to me had called Joe DiMattia and Jamie Douglas to find out if I was who I said I was, and I had the comfortable feeling that I was not a suspect in Abdul's death. I told everything I knew about Abdul and his connection to Shelley Gardner's cocaine, leaving out Val's involvement in the supplying of illegal substances. I had a few regrets about that. But I didn't think Valerie had killed either Abdul or Shelley, and I desperately wanted to protect Tori. It stunned me that I cared enough for her to put my own ass in a sling, but then again I was only on the Weldon case to be near her. My initial interest had been in Marsh Zeidler's safety, and once I had established that he was in no jeopardy I had only hung around to get an occasional shot from those green eyes or an occasional thrill up my back from that musical voice on the phone. The money helped, I suppose, but normally I give cases involving violence a wide berth, even though I am dragged into them kicking and screaming every so often. Skip-traces and divorces and missing persons are more my line, and insurance frauds and car repos, and if someone occasionally takes a swing at me, it happens infrequently enough for me not to consider another line of work.

Were my acting career healthier I would not be a private investigator. But the agency fills in the gaps in my bankbook, and helps me afford Laphroaig and standing rib roasts and books and plays and records and women like Tori Weldon. It also fills a need in me that I recognize as perverse. As much as I love the good life and the luxuries and the thrill of a good book or a good philosophical discussion, there is a part of me that is tremendously stimulated by danger, by the wild side, the dark underbelly of things that actors and storm-door salesmen and CPAs rarely encounter. Most people never get to venture much beyond their own milieu, be it that of insular wealth or suburban lethargy or the time-bomb danger of the mean city streets. But I have it all. Between my PI license and my Screen Actors Guild card, I am living my life full open, the variety of life's experiences are there for me to sample and to accept or leave alone. Unfortunately, I often get in deeper than I would like. Finding Abdul's two-day-old corpse was not one of the highlights of my life.

But Tori was, and I think I understood that my eagerness to bust this case was so I could strut and preen in front of her in some strange ritual mating dance; she'd be impressed with me and proud of me and grateful to me, and then maybe some day she'd love me. I was hooked, all right, and hurt by the wall that had sprung up between us since Shelley's death. I wanted to knock down that wall, brick by brick, and to do it I had to find the killer of Shelley and Abdul. Now, isn't that simple?

When I pulled into the lot at the office I saw Jo had already left, but I noticed Ray Tucek's car, and that made me nervous. I took the stairs two at a time. Ray was waiting for me at Jo's desk, reading a two-week-old *Time* magazine.

"Trouble in River City," he said as I walked in. "Where you been, son?"

"Finding bodies and then explaining to the law why they shouldn't book me for murder. What's wrong?"

"Whose body?"

"You first."

"Okay," he said. "The old man left the house this morning about ten o'clock, carrying a gym bag that says Oakland Raiders on it, which tells you how old it is. I tailed him to the airport. He went into the Aero Mexico terminal, and later he boarded a flight that took off at 1:40 P.M. for Bonita and Cabo San Lucas. Which one he was heading for I couldn't find out."

"Where the hell is Bonita?"

"Got a map?" he said.

I got down my world atlas, the one so old that by now most of the African nations have new names, and on the map of Mexico I quickly found Bonita with my thumbnail, about a fourth of the way down the Baja peninsula on the Sea of Cortez.

"From what I could find out at the airport," Ray said, "Bonita's just a herky-jerky fishing village. No one goes there except to fish for marlin."

I stared at the map until all of a sudden I got that prickling on the backs of my hands, and I slammed the atlas shut and said, "Ray, do me a favor. Call Aero Mexico and book me on the next flight to Bonita."

"Hell of a time to go fishing," he mumbled.

I went into my inner office and called Tori on the other line. "Why did you let your father leave town without telling me?"

"Leave town?" she said, and her astonishment sounded genuine enough. "He didn't leave town. He got dressed and shaved this morning and said he was going to play tennis. I thought it would be good for him to get out. He hasn't gone anywhere since . . . Shelley."

"He's somewhere now—Mexico."

"Mexico?"

"Listen carefully, Tori, it's very important. I want you to drive into town and pick up your sister Valerie right away. Don't take no for an answer. Take her out to my place. You remember how to get there?"

There was an embarrassed silence.

"Both of you stay there until you hear from me. Don't go out, don't answer the door unless you know who it is. I'll have Jo— Marsh Zeidler's wife—bring you out some groceries."

"But why?"

"Because Valerie's life is in danger and yours might be, too, and I want you taking good care of the woman I love. So just do it. I'll call the manager and have him let you in."

"I don't understand—"

136

"I have no time to explain, Tori. Just trust me, okay?" I hung up and went back into the outer office where Ray was just finishing up with Aero Mexico.

"Can I get to the airport in an hour forty-five?"

He looked at his watch. "At this time of night with the way you drive? Probably not."

"Good, it's settled then," I said. "You're driving."

By the time the plane took off it was that peculiar time of day between light and darkness, so early during the winter, that was not quite twilight and not quite dusk, but instead seemed to encourage introspection and self-search. The patchwork of lights that was Los Angeles from the air seemed endless as we roared out over the ocean, sharply turned left and headed toward the border. I was on the landward side of the plane and thus could appreciate the electrical patterns, the long moving ribbons of freeway, the random glowing patches of commercial areas and the carefully laid-out residential tracts. It all reminded me of when I'd first journeyed to Hollywood from Chicago and rented a bachelor pad high in the Hollywood Hills, from whose balcony I could look out over the city and shake my fist and say "Big town, I'll get you yet." That I never did is not germane here.

The plane was just one-third full; only a few hardy souls were anxious to go billfishing in December, to sit on flying bridges drinking Tecate and fighting their fiberglass fishing rods until their shoulders went beyond aching, fantasizing they were Papa Hemingway and murmuring things like, "Oh, Great Fish, I love you, Fish." I figured I was unique on the plane as one winging southward to prevent a murder.

I thought about what I had. Whoever was supplying Abdul with cocaine had killed Shelley with the strychnine meant for Buck, and then snuffed Abdul to keep him from talking. Valerie swore she didn't know who the connection was but the connection didn't know that, and I wanted her out of her apartment and safe in mine, and Tori with her. I had Buck in Mexico, and if he was there for the reason I thought, I had a motive. All I didn't have was a killer.

* * *

There were two hotels in Bonita, Tweedledee and -dum both facing the beach where the warm waters of the Gulf of California lapped at the dirty white sand, and the smell of salt and fish hung in the air like that of hot dogs at a warm July ballgame. I checked both hotels to see if Buck Weldon were registered, but I didn't really expect to find him there. The hotel I chose for myself enjoyed my patronage because it was painted white to the other's dirty pink. It had few amenities, catering as it did to the macho sportsman who had no need for frills such as room service and air conditioning. Across the beamed ceiling of the flyspecked little lobby there was one mournful strand of silver tinsel to remind us that the festival of the birth of Christ was close at hand. At one end of the lobby there was a bar the size of those once found on railroad club cars, but no bartender. Apparently that function was performed by the desk clerk, a white-haired little man with a potbelly and an accent alarmingly like Frank Sinatra's in *The Pride and the Passion,* who apologized that because of my late arrival with no advance reservation, all the fishing boats for tomorrow were booked.

"I'll just learn the countryside, then," I said. "Any picturesque little towns around here I can visit?"

"Little towns, señor?"

"Yes."

"I don't think so. La Negra. Los Santos, maybe."

"Where are they?"

"Where are they, señor? In the hills."

"Which way is Los Santos, for instance?"

"There is nothing in Los Santos, señor."

"*Sí—yo comprendo.* But—*donde está Los Santos?*"

As though he were giving me the declension of a Latin verb with no understanding of why I might want it, the clerk gave me halting directions to Los Santos.

"And La Negra?"

"*Ai,* La Negra is very small, señor. Twenty people, perhaps. *No más.*"

"Yes, but where is it?"

La Negra turned out to be in the opposite direction from Los Santos, but I dutifully noted his directions.

"Can I rent a car tomorrow? Or are they all booked in advance, too?"

138

"Rent a car?"

"Yes. *Sí*. I want to rent a car."

"We have no cars to rent, señor. There is a taxi, perhaps, but I don't think he'll go to no Los Santos."

I sighed. It had been a hard day. "Do *you* have a car?"

"Me?"

"Yes. I'll give you fifty dollars for the use of your car tomorrow, and another fifty if I need it the next day."

His eyes lit up—that was probably a week's salary. "My car?"

His habit of repeating whatever I said was beginning to irritate me. "I'll pick it up at about eight o'clock tomorrow morning, and when I bring it back I'll fill the gas tank." I fished in my pocket and pulled out twenty dollars. I've found, to my rue, that those twenties come in awfully handy. It used to be, in the dear lost days of Sam Spade and Philip Marlowe, that a five-dollar bill could buy you just about anything, from information to a high-class hooker. Alas, times change, and Dashiell Hammett probably wouldn't understand about *Hustler* magazine and video game arcades either. "As a deposit, okay?"

The clerk moved like a mongoose to put the money away, and I followed his directions down the paint-peeled hallway. He told me to turn right, and I found out later he'd erred and should have said left. I hoped his directions to Los Santos were better.

The next morning the clerk's *carro* turned out to be not a Chevy but a Plymouth Duster, of such a vintage that, had it been a bottle of wine, it would have cost more than it did as a car. The clerk kindly showed me the little tricks he had to get it started, and pretty soon I was bucketing off down the two-lane highway south. Bitterly I noted how the cotton batting from the torn upholstery was sticking to my dark blue slacks.

The sea beside me was gray-blue in the overcast, broken by occasional whitecaps. It was migration season for the gray whale of California, that time of year when the entire herd swims down from the Arctic to mate and calve in the warmer waters of the Gulf of California, and I tried catching a glimpse or two of the genial monsters as they broke the surface for air, or at least a telltale spume of spray. Nothing is more stirring than the sight of those immense tail flukes coming out of the water and waving a friendly hello, but I didn't get to see much, mainly because I was busy avoiding the potholes on the rarely traveled highway.

I found the turn-off road for Los Santos as the clerk had promised, although calling it a road at all was hyperbole. It was more of a firebreak through the ground cover, heading upward into the foothills at a startling angle. The hills were brown and sere, with only an occasional clump of scrub grass or weeds to break the monotony, and the wind created little dust devils that danced along just inches above the ground only to finally commit seppuku against the random outcrop of boulder. The little Plymouth groaned and shook, and I pulled the choke almost all the way out to keep it from surrendering to gravitational pull and sliding backward into the ocean. There were other tire tracks in the dirt, and I prayed I wouldn't meet another car coming down and be forced into a Robin Hood-and-Little John-on-the-bridge confrontation that I was bound to lose. If there was any animal life in these hills near the roadside it was not readily apparent to the passing motorist, as if even the prairie dogs were ashamed to admit they had the bad judgment to live here.

After a few miles the road mercifully leveled off and turned southward, and I found myself once more on paved highway. I estimated my climb to have been some six hundred feet. It was cooler up here, and the desolation of the landscape was now dotted by pitiful shacks and sad little victory gardens and vegetable patches or by a rusting pickup truck. Scattered raggedy children looked up with curiosity as I passed, and then the incidence of inhabited structures grew more frequent, and after another two miles I reached what passed in these parts for civilization: a two-pump gas station, general store, and post office, all under one slanty-down roof. I had reached Los Santos. The Pearl of the Baja, no doubt. The dog who greeted me on the porch was either the mangiest mongrel I'd ever seen, or the mayor. Or both.

Inside I purchased a bottle of Dos Equis for two dollars and what I wanted to know for another ten. I had guessed right, thus saving myself a trip to La Negra. The fat lady in the store seemed happy to get my money, and I did what she told me and drove a few miles farther down the road and then peeled off the tarmac onto a cattle path, and I thought if my hunch had been wrong I would have felt like the leading candidate for the title of Horse's Patoot of the Half-Century.

In another mile I found the cabin. It seemed newer and perhaps more substantial than others I had passed in the neighborhood. It had a concrete foundation, for one thing, and it had been painted some time since the election of Eisenhower. Next to it was a four-year-old Jeep Wagoneer with California license plates. I drove past the Jeep about three hundred yards and parked in a copse of trees, then walked back along the path to the cabin. There was cholla cactus and pokeweed underfoot, and the dust made the inside of my nose feel dirty.

I stepped up on the jerry-built front porch so that the boards squeaked, and knocked on the door firmly. Then I listened. Inside there was someone stirring, a chair scraped against the floor, and stockinged feet padded toward the door. It opened, and Buck Weldon stood blinking into the sunshine, a look of surprise on his face, and more than surprise, chagrin.

"Good morning, Mr. Kale," I said.

○ **12** ○

"Oh, you bastard!" Buck said, and there was no malice in it, only an infinite sadness. "Saxon, you son of a bitch!"

He turned and went back into the cabin, his shoulders slumping like Willy Loman in *Death of a Salesman,* his emotional sample cases dragging him down, too. He didn't bother slamming the door in my face, so I took it as an invitation to come in. The cabin was one room, plus a small john and a kitchenette, and was furnished with a double bed, a sturdy oak dining table and chairs, which also doubled as a work area, a sofa that was ancient but comfortable, and a chest of drawers. It wasn't exactly the kind of place you'd want to move into and set up housekeeping in, but it was certainly livable for a few days at a time for a no-frills guy like Buck Weldon.

He sat down dejectedly on the edge of the bed, hands folded between his knees and his head down, leaving me in the middle of the room, awkward and intruding. I finally sat down at the dining table. No one said anything, and ions of tension were bouncing all over the room like gnats at a picnic. Then Buck looked up at me, righteous anger and deep disappointment further flushing his ruddy complexion. "You have no right," he said. "You had no right."

"I'm sorry, Buck."

"How did you find out?"

"The day after Marsh Zeidler got shot at in front of your house, your daughter hired me to look after you. And to find out who was trying to kill you." His frown deepened at the cut to his pride but I rode right over anything he might be getting ready to say. "I poked around and talked to everyone who's in your life, Buck, and I found out a lot of interesting things. Buck Weldon and Jack Kale have the same agent, the same publisher, and they each seem to write a book every two years—alternate years. Every time you finished a Bart Steele novel you locked yourself in your den and wrote furiously for another year and never let anyone read what you were doing, even Tori. Even the name is a giveaway when you think about it. I'm sure you got the name Buck because of your prowess with the ladies. But Buck is also a slang word for dollar. Jack is slang for money. And Kale—kale is a leafy green vegetable like cabbage—and cabbage is also slang for money. It fits, Buck."

He nodded.

"I hired a bodyguard for you—he's been with you since the beginning of the week. He tailed you to the airport yesterday and when I'd heard you'd gone to Mexico all the other pieces started falling together." I took the autographed copy of *The Avenging Angel* out of my pocket and showed him his photograph on the back cover. "The lady at the store down the road said she recognized this picture and gave me directions where to find you."

He was quiet for a moment, digesting, feeling betrayed and exposed and, I suppose, humiliated and foolish, and then he sighed a noisy exhalation and stood up. "As long as you're here," he said, "you might as well have some coffee. It's just fresh this morning."

He went to the stove where an old-fashioned aluminum per-

142

colator stood, and got down two cups that didn't match. He poured the coffees and served them black without asking how I preferred it. Maybe he remembered, or maybe he didn't care. Then he went and sat back down on the bed, chewing his lip, lost in thought. I didn't want to intrude so I just waited and drank my coffee, which was strong with the flavor of chicory.

"I suppose," he finally said, "you want to know why? Why the mystery, the subterfuge, the two names and all?"

"I have to admit my curiosity's killing me."

"Your curiosity is killing me, too," he said. He took a cigarette from the crumpled pack in his shirt pocket and lighted it, took a deep drag and coughed prodigiously, that wheezing baritone smoker's cough which I knew I'd have in twenty years if I didn't stop or cut down on my smoking. Then he wiped his eyes and sniffed, and said, "I'm a writer, kid, a good one. I always wanted to write, even in grade school. I wrote compositions and little short stories about dogs who saved little boys from grizzly bears—shit like that. As I matured, so did my stories, naturally. After college, I worked as a shoe salesman days and wrote nights, that's how badly I wanted it. Sold a couple of magazine pieces, just enough to keep the carrot dangling, just enough to know that somewhere out there was a market for my stories, for what I had to say inside.

"I got married, I had a little daughter, Tori, I was tired of scraping and kissing ass for dimes, I wrote a little potboiler that I thought was commercial as hell. *Cobalt Blue* was the name of it."

"The first adventure of Bart Steele," I said.

"Bart Steele—what a ludicrous name for a pretty ludicrous guy. He fucked everything that walked, bashed in faces first and talked later, had a code of ethics somewhere to the right of Attila, and he was practically invincible—the only thing he couldn't do was leap tall buildings at a single bound. *Cobalt Blue* was a comic strip in prose. That's all it was ever meant to be."

"None of this is exactly hard news, Buck."

"Keep your pants on, I'm telling you how it got to be like it is. Okay, so Bart Steele was a bigger hit than anything I'd ever imagined. Remember, life was a lot simpler back in those days. You couldn't buy spread-beaver pictures at your corner newsstand, a porno movie was something you rented from an old guy on the corner with a yellow beard and dirt under his fingernails, and in the regular movies there was a Production Code so that violence was something you hinted at, not saw. Life was quieter then, a little more straitlaced. And *Cobalt Blue,* for its day, was pretty hot stuff. It blew through the country like a wind—without Bart Steele, things might be different today in books and movies. I was a pioneer. Of course, somebody was bound to do it."

"But you did it. And you got rich."

"Not right away—but richer than I ever thought I'd be. But I'm a dreamer, son, under all the macho bullshit I'm a dreamer. I thought now that I had a little fuck-you money I could do what I really wanted. I wrote another book—a sensitive story about a man and a farm and his love of the land and how he and his farm and his children grew up with America during the first part of this century. It was a hell of a book."

"I don't recall it, Buck."

"That's because it never got published. Went right into the shitter. Jeremy Radisson said it wasn't what the reading public expected from Buck Weldon. They expected big titties and brass knuckles and sweat and sperm and bourbon neat with no chaser, and he said they'd never forgive me if I didn't give them that. So I wrote another Bart Steele, and it was even bigger than the first one. Number-one best-seller. Little boys used to take the paperback version into the bathroom with them and beat off to the juicy parts."

I laughed nervously, remembering my own childhood and how I'd kept that very book hidden from the nuns at Saint Al's.

"Then after a while," he went on, "I realized that I was trapped. Trapped by success. I'd never be able to write anything except blood and violence and sex as long as the public had Buck Weldon and Bart Steele all bound together in their minds. I'd never be able to write anything important. So I wrote *Silver Mountain* and I used the byline Jack V. Kale."

"What's the *V* for?"

"You're not the detective you ought to be, son," he said with a triumphant chuckle. "Even Bart Steele would have figured that out. My mother didn't name me Buck, for God's sake. My first name is Virgil. My daughters, Victoria and Valerie—"

I accepted defeat graciously. "I should have put that together, too," I said. "Next time, Buck."

He took a noisy slurp of his hot coffee. "Anyway," he said, "I sent the book to Elliot Knaepple under the name Kale. He was a good agent, even though he's one of the sleaziest little pricks I've ever had the misfortune to meet. After a few months I casually mentioned if he'd gotten anything good in over the transom and he told me about this great novel by some writer down in Mexico and I asked to read it, and then I told him it was the best thing I'd ever read and I pushed him to sell it. I even called Radisson after Elliot had submitted it to him and put in a commercial for it, and Radisson published it. I didn't think it would sell very well, I just did it for the satisfaction. But lo and behold, it wins the National Book Award for that year, and a whole truckload of other prizes, too. Critics raved, customers bought, and what I had hoped would be a succès d'estime was a major hit."

"Why didn't you come forward then and admit you'd written it?"

"Because I realized I could have it both ways. I could write what I wanted and make money, and I could grind out the murder stuff like sausages and make even more money. Besides, I'd gotten kind of fond of old Bart Steele. He was the other side of me, the side that I wished I'd had—all-American hero."

"But you never told Radisson or Knaepple? Or even your children?"

He leaned back, one elbow digging into the pillow behind him, some of the old Weldon cockiness coming through loud and clear. "I thought it was a hoot," he said. "I was putting on the whole world. I liked it. I liked reading stories about Jack V. Kale, the Mystery Man of American Letters. I had my fame as Buck Weldon, I had lots of money from both Weldon and Kale, and I had more inner joy, more *naches,* if you understand Yiddish, than I'll ever be able to tell you about. So I bought this little cabin and rented a post office box down the road and I've lived fairly happily ever after."

"And nobody knows?"

"Not until you stuck your nose in, no. Just the two of us in this room."

"You're wrong, I'm afraid," I said. "Somebody else knows, too—and they're trying to kill you because of it. They killed Shelley by mistake—that poisoned cocaine was meant for you."

His lips went white when I mentioned Shelley, but it was a passing thing, a flicker, and he got it under control right away. "How do you figure it's because of Jack Kale?"

"Because I can't find anyone that has a reason for killing Buck Weldon."

"Lots of people might," he said. "I've got my problems with a lot of people."

"Sure you do," I said, "but none with a big enough motive to kill."

"Radisson. I'm suing him for half a million."

"And he'll pay off, Buck. It's a lot cheaper than losing the author who made him a millionaire in the first place. He'll settle, and gladly."

"My son-in-law," he said. "My ex-son-in-law. He hates my guts."

"That he does. I've spoken to him."

"Do you know what I did to him?"

I nodded. "And he had it coming. But he's not a killer."

"How can you be so sure?"

"Buck," I said, "I was in the army once—when I was a kid just out of college. I was one of the lucky ones they didn't send to Nam. I fought the battle of Augusta, Georgia, as a television writer and producer at Fort Gordon. But I went through basic training like everyone else—the hazing, the hassling—and it really does separate the men from the boys. I remember in our platoon there was a bully. Ramsford was his name—a big old Bohunk from someplace in Ohio. He was older than most of us—middle twenties, I guess. He'd been in the service before, in the Marine Corps, no less. He'd pulled a tour and gotten out, but he couldn't hack it in civilian life because he didn't have anybody to kill. What is it they used to say NCO stood for? 'No Chance Outside'? Anyway he came back in—to the army this time. But he'd stayed away too long and couldn't get his grade back, so he was a recruit just like the rest of us, and went all through basic training again. You can imagine how terrified we all were of him. We were kids off the campus, kids just out of high school, kids who still thought if you jag off you get pimples. And here was a guy who had killed people in Vietnam. He knew it and he used it—they made him the platoon guide because of his experience. He bullied us all equally, without regard to race, color or creed, and we all took it and hoped he wouldn't hurt us. But there was this one kid in particular— Harvey Lapinsky from Jackson Heights, Queens. He was Jewish and an intellectual, and he was also fat and nearsighted and shy and all the other unathletic and unmacho things that really bring out the savagery in a guy like Ramsford. So Ramsford made poor Harvey his special project. He was always on him about something—if it wasn't military, it was about Harvey's inability to do twenty push-ups without stopping to rest in the middle, or about Harvey's slightly effete way of doing things, or he'd make jokes about the size of Harvey's dick, which I have to admit almost didn't show at all in the showers, or about Harvey's tits which were about a B-cup. And when Ramsford ran out of other things there was always the old standby—'You dirty Jew bastard, you killed Christ!' Basic training is the pits for everybody, but for Harvey Lapinsky it was a particular brand of hell. Even guys in the platoon that didn't like Harvey started feeling sorry for him, but Ramsford wouldn't let up, and there was no one of the rest of us that felt good enough about himself to try and make him."

"I get the picture," Buck said. "Not the point, but the picture."

"Well," I said, "one fine day after two hours of PE and seven more of marching and drilling, and a one-hour block of instruction on what to do if you're captured by the enemy and tortured, we were all sitting around cleaning our rifles. The army is very big on that, having a clean rifle. Having a clean floor. Having a clean company area with no cigarette butts. They made you take a crap in the middle of the room with no doors or partitions, but by God, your rifle was clean. Anyway, on this particular evening Ramsford was going after poor Harvey with a vengeance. He was sitting on his foot locker with his M-1 in pieces on his lap, and he said something to Harvey. I forget what it was—it doesn't matter, really, because it was the last straw. And Harvey walked over to him with his own rifle in his hands and he smashed the butt of it right into Ramsford's mouth. Hard as he could. Now, maybe that wasn't as hard as the rest of us might have been able to do it, but it was hard enough—right in the mouth. And Ramsford just sat there with a stunned expression on his face—and then he opened his mouth to say something and all his teeth fell out. Just like in a 'Road Runner' cartoon. And he looked down at his lap which was covered with broken teeth and rifle parts, and then he passed out."

"You are a windy bastard," Buck said. "Will you get to the meat?"

"I just got to it, Buck. Nobody would blow the whistle on Harvey about what happened, not even Ramsford, and after that every time Harvey walked in the door Ramsford almost peed in his pants. He'd hide—actually hide in the latrine or outside or in the boiler room whenever Harvey was around. He was still an asshole, and he was still big enough and tough enough to break Harvey's back with two fingers, but he didn't. He couldn't. He was a broken man after that. And I guarantee you, Buck, after what you did to Deke James last year, he's just like Ramsford. I hit him and he didn't try to hit me back. He pulled a gun on me and I backed him down. Deke has the motive to kill you, all right—but he doesn't have the backbone any more. Big tough pro football player—but you broke him."

Buck got up and poured us some more coffee, and we drank it and smoked cigarettes and were quiet for a while, both of us with our own thoughts. Then Buck turned his head quickly and looked at me, almost the way a bird turns its head. "Nobody even knows Jack V. Kale," he said. "Why should they want to kill him?"

"If I knew why, Buck, I'd know who. But whoever it is will figure out where you are and be down here after you."

"And what do we do then?"

"Hopefully," I said, "we take him."

Buck looked at his watch. It was coming on to noon. "Let's go," he said, "it's lunchtime. I'm buying." We started out to the Jeep.

I said, "Aren't you going to lock the door?"

"I never lock—oh, yeah, under the circumstances . . ." He went back and locked up the cabin. As we got in the Jeep he smiled to himself and said, "Have I your permission to use that bit?"

"What bit?"

"About the guy's teeth coming out like in a cartoon. That sounds just like something Bart Steele might do."

We drove down to the general store—what Buck referred to as the Los Santos Civic Center—and bought a loaf of bread, some beer, some cheese and chorizo sausage, and went back to the cabin and consumed them and swapped old army stories and old detective stories, and it gave me a jolt when I thought that we might be doing this lots of other times, father-in-law to son-in-law, but I had to put that out of my mind, there were other more pressing matters to attend to.

After lunch Buck said he always took a long walk about this time and invited me to join him. "Back in LA we don't exercise enough. We drive to the mailbox, for Christ's sake. That's just one of the things I like about coming here. I walk in the fresh air, I get my heart started and my blood moving, and I *think*. I clear all the crap out of my head, no phones and no cars and no bullshit. It revitalizes me."

We were walking in what amounted to a small forest, hilly terrain far from the road, up where it was so quiet you could hear through the branches of loblolly pine the wings of a hawk as it whirled two hundred feet above your head. When the wind was right you could also hear the distant rumble of the ocean, several miles away. There was a peace there that could never be found on Sunset Boulevard. It was good.

Buck wasn't even puffing, but I was winded from the up-and-downhill walking, which Buck executed at a more than brisk pace. He carried a blackthorn walking stick and wore a little canvas hat with a stingy brim, and had a red and black lumberjacket which made him look as though he'd been born to these hills and not in the urban congestion of the East Coast. We talked about his writing a lot, and it fascinated me to hear how a simple story like my Ramsford-Harvey tale could be the germination of an entire book. We talked about alcohol—I was a Scotch man and a brandy man, while he was strictly bourbon. We talked about the real differences between the insurance and divorce work that paid my bills and the fictionalized exploits of "private eyes." And we talked about Tori.

"Is there something going on there I don't know about?" he said.

"You know about it, Buck. I think I love her."

"You think. Hah! That's the best there is, thinking you do. You're never sure, because nobody knows what love really is. It's more than hormones, I tell you that."

We had wound through the hills to a rocky arroyo, hidden from the view of practically everyone except the overhead hawk. There was a sheer drop of about sixty feet, at the bottom of which was a stand of boulders and cactus and weeds and the tiniest trickle of a stream which came from somewhere in the rocks and disappeared into a similar crevice on the other side of the arroyo before it headed presumably to the sea. I didn't wonder it was the place where Buck came to clear out his head.

"Sit down," he said.

We sat in the dirt, our backs against two rocks. It was almost soothing to listen to the sounds that the silence made.

He didn't look at me. "There's something you ought to understand about Tori. Tori was born without any defenses. Like that boy in the plastic bubble—only he had no protection from disease. Tori has no protection from hurt. So much so that when things go wrong, like her marriage, like a lot of things in her life, instead of bouncing back like most of us, Tori gets to thinking that she somehow deserves it, deserves the hurt. And sometimes, if something is good—she'll find a way to turn it back on herself so that it self-destructs. You understand?"

"Wouldn't it be easier to say 'Stay away from my daughter' and get it over with?"

"I'm not telling you that, damn it. You're a straightforward guy, you would probably be damn good for her. I'm just telling you, though, that you might be in for a difficult time, the both of you."

"Maybe," I said. "But when you really care about someone, aren't you supposed to take the good with the bad? Get through the bad times by supporting each other and then ride on top of the waves when it's good?"

"You're an old-fashioned romantic, aren't you? Well, go for it, son, I wouldn't want to stop you. Just be careful of hurting her, you hear? Remember Deke James? I think you know what I'll do if you hurt her."

"I probably will at some point, Buck. You can't help hurting someone sometimes, you do it because it never occurs to you that a little thing like that—whatever it is, is going to hurt. We all hurt each other. I think the object of the game, though, is to try your damnedest not to."

We listened to the birds twitter and to the bugs and lizards scurrying through the leaves and the dust, and Buck said, "Hurting someone without knowing it—I guess I've done that."

I looked over at him, but he was just reflecting. An answer didn't seem to be required.

"I guess I've hurt somebody so bad without even knowing it, that they want me dead. That's a pretty scary thing. Makes you want to stay in bed with your head under the covers. Or hide out—like Tori does."

"You can't live like that, Buck. Keeping out the hurt just keeps out the good stuff, too. We all have to take our chances—you, me, Tori. You just have to hope all the times you're dealt a really crappy hand that the name of the game is lowball."

He grinned a crooked grin at me. "Not bad for a layman," he said. And then his look turned serious and he inched a bit closer to me. "I need for you to promise me something."

"I won't hurt Tori."

"That's good—but not what I was going to ask you. I want your word that if we get out of here with our necks that you won't tell anyone about me—about Jack Kale."

"It's that important to you?"

"It's my life," he said simply, and the saying of it was so earnest that I shivered involuntarily.

"Shelley is gone, now," he went on, "and I'm too old and beat up and tired to find another one. My daughters are grown, they don't really need me any more. All I've got is my work. Not the Buck Weldon work, that's easy. The Jack Kale work. It's my life."

"You have my word, then, Buck. I won't even tell Tori if you don't want me to."

We shook hands solemnly. "You're a good man. Remember I told you I liked you right off?"

"Yes," I said, "but it was close. Just think, I might have told you I thought Jack Kale's writing stunk."

We both drove back to Bonita that evening, and I returned the desk clerk's car to him with the remainder of his money. I also checked out of the hotel, Buck having insisted I bunk down on the sofa in the cabin. He pointed out that Tori was paying my expenses on this case, and that indirectly meant that he was, and he was goddamned if he was going to keep me in a hotel when there was a perfectly serviceable sofa going begging. I think he really didn't want to be alone with the possibility of a killer hunting him down in his bed but was too proud to say so. That suited me fine. I didn't want Buck alone either.

We had dinner at the other hotel—it had a small dining room and the *camarones* were surprisingly good. I can't say the same for their wine list, however, and I wound up drinking beer with my dinner. Buck stayed with his bourbon, drunk neat, pointing out that if you were going to put ice cubes in your drink in Mexico it was just like drinking the water.

When we got back to the cabin he said, "I don't suppose a straight arrow like you has any dope on you?"

I wasn't sure if he was kidding. When I saw he wasn't I said, "No, I don't believe in it."

"Neither do I, that's the funny part. It's one of those things you get into because everyone else is, and then you're there and you don't see any real good reason for stopping, and pretty soon it's just what you do. Well, it's just as well." He kicked off his boots and sat down on the bed. "Me for turning in," he said. "You want to stay up and read, the light won't bother me."

"No, thanks. But I think I'd like to walk off my dinner. Out where we were this afternoon, maybe. I've got some thinking I need to do."

"About what?"

"That's the really neat thing about thinking, Buck," I said. "You don't have to tell."

He went barefoot to his Oakland Raiders bag and pulled out a flashlight and handed it to me. "Here, you'll need this. You think you can find your way back?"

"There's never any going back, Buck."

It took me about fifteen minutes to get there. The sky was clear and the moon was nearly full, so I had no trouble finding my way. There was a breeze up here on this plateau above the sea, and I turned the collar of my jacket up against it. It wasn't exactly cold, but enough to make you think about it.

I lighted a cigarette and listened to the sounds of the stream at the bottom of the arroyo, coming up to me in the still night like an echo of itself, and I thought. I thought about Tori and her hang-ups, about whether someone had given them to her or whether they'd come as original equipment, but it didn't matter, because Tori had moved me in a way no one else ever had, certainly not Leila, for whom everything from job to sex to cooking a meal was goal-oriented. Beyond the thoroughly natural and delightful lust I felt for Tori was something that touched my core and made me want to be with her and stand by her and help her face life with a smile and a jutting-out chin, to warm and protect her and yet allow her to function independently of me, to keep that elusive quality of "space" for each of us on the outer edges of us where our spaces did not touch each other. I wasn't sure I could handle it. I was only sure I wanted to.

And then I thought about Buck, and his giant put-on of the world for all these years. I guess he enjoyed getting away with it, just the way anything proscribed is more fun. No cigarette ever tasted better than the ones sneaked in the boys' room at Saint Aloysuis under the scrutiny of the sisters; no sex was better than that undertaken on a girl's front porch with her father ten feet away in the living room reading his paper; no feeling was greater than having dared and won. And Buck was a winner, one of the few, the best part being that he'd done it on his own terms. That was everyone's dream, to have it all ways—one had to envy those few who did it.

And then it all came clear to me so that my skin literally tingled with excitement, and I flipped my half-smoked cigarette over the edge of the drop-off and watched it fall crazily through space, dancing with the air currents that eddied around the arroyo walls until it disappeared into the blackness, and I took the flashlight from my pocket and switched it on, hardly able to wait to get back to the cabin to tell Buck I knew who was trying to kill him and why, and as I started to turn around something hit me incredibly hard on the side of the head and all of a sudden I disappeared into the blackness, too.

○ 13 ○

The first thing I felt was cold and darkness. That was before I tried to move my head and a fifty-megaton nuclear warhead went off inside my skull, and with it the realization that someone had tied my hands behind my back and that there wasn't a hell of a lot of blood circulating through my fingers. I opened my eyes, but that didn't help much because I was lying facedown in some grass or weeds or something and there wasn't a whole lot to see. I started wriggling, trying to get my weight shifted so that I could sit up, and then I felt strong hands gripping my shoulders, pulling at me, getting me sitting upright so I could see the sky and the stars and the moon and the silhouette of a large man with broad shoulders against the night sky. I couldn't see who it was, but I knew anyway.

And when he said, "Wake up, Mr. Saxon," and I heard the light underlay, the barest suggestion of Swedish accent, there was no doubt at all in my mind, the lilt, the up-and-down rhythm of Scandinavia, and while there was a two-second lull in the pain in my head I said, "Hello, Professor Kullander."

He nodded in satisfaction that I was all right. As my vision cleared I was able to see his face better. He looked troubled, bemused, almost as though he were listening to a piece of classical music he couldn't quite identify as Mozart or Haydn or Franz Liszt. He began stuffing a pipe with tobacco from a soft leather pouch, and then he lighted it with a wooden match, and the yellow flame illuminated his face even more. He could have been in his office or his study at home, having an after-dinner pipe before correcting some term papers.

"I suppose you're wondering why I didn't just kill you?" Bo Kullander said.

"Not exactly wondering. Grateful."

"I'm sorry. I am going to kill you—I have to, you see. But I had to talk to you first."

"Why?"

"If you discovered the secret of Jack Kale then someone else might. I wanted to make sure my tracks were covered. I hope you'll oblige me by explaining."

"I see. What if I don't?"

He clamped the pipe stem between his teeth and took a few steps forward, like a place kicker, and smashed his hiking boot into my face. I was able to turn away so that the sole simply scraped most of the skin off my cheek, and the impact sent me rolling backward over onto my back; I rolled over several times in the dust. When I stopped Kullander came over and gently sat me up again.

"Are you all right?" he asked solicitously. I could only nod.

"It's up to you, Mr. Saxon, in what manner you die. I can make it very quick and painless for you, or I can beat you to death, slowly and methodically. You must choose."

My voice came out like Kirk Douglas's, strained and squeezed. "All right." I nodded my head to let him know I was willing to talk to him, and I sucked in the chill air as if any minute there wouldn't be any more, and come to think of it there was more than a little truth in that. Kullander waited patiently until I was composed enough to talk in a relatively normal fashion again. I began to.

"I think you made your mistake by bungling your first three murder attempts," I said. "That got people interested."

"What people?" he said. "You?"

"Me, the police. But when I started sifting through Buck's life I began noticing the similarities. And you helped me out a great deal, too."

"I?"

"When I saw you in your office you said something I found terribly interesting at the time. You said Buck often writes with a scalpel—so sharp that the words can cause pain."

"I did. I believe that."

"And then on the phone you said the same thing about Jack Kale."

He puffed. "Careless of me."

"Not terribly. But it helped me to figure out that Buck was wearing two hats. Once I had that doped out I narrowed it down to the fact that it was Jack Kale in danger and not Buck, if you understand. So I came down here to protect Jack Kale. I'm not doing a very good job of it."

"Careless of *you*," he said.

"I hope you're a better writer than a murderer, Professor. You screwed this one up badly. Three attempts at a killing and no cigar. The cocaine was a bad idea. It meant you were going to have to kill Abdul Muhammad as well."

"Small loss," he said. "Abdul was an insect, a leech, living off women and spewing his Black Supremacy filth—I enjoyed that, even. As for Miss Gardner, I deeply regret that mistake. She was not terribly bright but she was a nice woman."

"And all out of envy, too." His eyebrows lifted imperceptibly. "You told me yourself, Kullander, that you were a frustrated novelist. Those that can, do. Those that can't, teach. It ground you really hard that Buck Weldon, a man you considered a reactionary, a philistine and a lightweight, could write the way Jack Kale did. You doped it out early on—you told me you were a literary detective. So when you realized no one else in the world knew who Jack Kale was, you thought you could kill Buck Weldon, and the next Jack V. Kale book would be written by you. I wouldn't be surprised if it isn't sitting in your desk drawer right now, done in copycat style. And then you step forward and confess that all these years it's been Professor Bo Kullander writing under the name of Jack V. Kale. You get the glory and the money and all the National Book Awards that have been piling up in Jeremy Radisson's office all these years, and you never again have to worry about your books not getting published because you're a built-in name, a winner, a literary giant. In the meantime Buck Weldon is dead and no one else is the wiser."

He narrowed his eyes at me for a moment. I could smell the aroma of his pipe. "Very good, Mr. Saxon. Very astute."

"Except you'll never pull it off. Too many people have died already. You'll never get away with two more."

"Of course I will, Mr. Saxon. Think of it a while. We are in a remote corner in Mexico. At this moment we are miles away from any sort of civilization. I plan to leave both you and Buck at the bottom of this arroyo where no one will ever dream of looking for you, where no one will find you by mistake. As far as the authorities in Los Angeles are concerned, you are two more missing persons. And as for the Mexican police, they'll never know. You are checked out of your hotel, and there is no reason they would look for you."

"There are several people who know where I am."

"Of what consequence to me, though? If the whole world knows where you are, or even if they find you? I didn't fly down here, I drove down, and there is no record of my crossing the border, because as you know at the checkpoint the Mexican officials just slow you down and ask how long you'll be in Mexico. I even neglected to purchase Mexican car insurance. So even on the off chance you are found, you and Weldon, no one can possibly connect me with your deaths. I taught a class yesterday morning. I've been where I should have at all times. I'm going to make it look as though you and Weldon killed each other, so it's unlikely anyone will look further than that."

"There's one part of it that I'm puzzled about, Professor, if you'll humor me. Abdul and the cocaine. How did that come about?"

"It was fairly easy. I knew who Abdul was around the campus, and I also knew his relationship to Valerie Weldon. I simply befriended him. You know, Sweden and socialism and Abdul's revolutionary schemes, it all seemed to fit in. At first I did so just because it was another angle that I might be able to use eventually. The brainstorm about the cocaine came later, when I learned from Buck himself that he was into fairly heavy drug use. Around a large university obtaining drugs is easier than buying a meatloaf sandwich, and I simply offered them to Abdul at a price so ridiculously low he couldn't resist. He was taking a huge commission off the top anyway, naturally, because he was greedy as well as coarse and stupid." He smiled, remembering. "After Miss Gardner's death he attempted a clumsy blackmail scheme."

"And that's why you killed him?"

"Oh, no, I was going to kill him anyway. The blackmail made me do it without much regret." He began pacing slowly, as if delivering a lecture on Nathaniel Hawthorne. "I do have regrets about you, Saxon, and certainly about Buck Weldon. He is a lovely man. But I have little choice. I *am* a good writer, and I can write as well as Kale, better, even. No one would ever give me a chance. Now they will."

I said, "Thousands of people out there can write, Kullander. Some make it and some don't. It has little to do with talent—it's luck and persistence and something else intangible."

"I know, Saxon. It's the intangible that I'm doing now. I'm making it happen. Capitalizing on a situation that is totally unique. It's my ticket up and out, and I have to take it. Especially now after Abdul and Miss Gardner—there is no turning back."

Had it been twenty minutes ago that I'd said that to Buck Weldon? Longer? Twenty years? Time was jumbled up, maybe because it was running out. I didn't know any more, but I knew that if Bo Kullander was going to kill me, I would not go gentle.

All the time we had been talking I was trying to work my hands free behind my back, but had only managed to make the ropes bite that much tighter into my wrists. I was in a sitting position now, my knees bent and my feet flat on the ground. Kullander was about ten feet from me, one foot up on a small rock, one hand braced on his thigh and the other cradling the bowl of his briar pipe.

He said, "I called Tori Weldon last night and she said her father had gone to Mexico and you after him. Of course I knew where— I've checked this site out before, you see. I knew you had solved the mystery of Jack Kale. Oh, I was angry, Saxon. You were not in my plans. So I drove down here early this morning—it took about four hours, but it was a pleasant drive. And I waited. Until you were alone. It's lucky you're such a night owl or I might have had to wait clear until tomorrow to kill you."

It was amazing how matter-of-fact he was being, as though he were talking about the weather or the plot of some novel he was reviewing for class instead of about killing two people. He was a cool one, was Bo Kullander.

"I'm sorry," he said, "that I had to hurt you before. But I needed to know. Now I do. I'll make it very quick."

He knocked his pipe ashes out against the heel of his hand and sucked on the pipestem noisily to make sure no wet dottle was clogging the airway. Then he put it in his pocket and walked over to me to break my neck.

When he got in front of me I rolled backward, a medium-size stone digging painfully into my back, and I shot my feet forward, ankles together, as hard as I could. They caught him in the left knee and he howled in pain as he stumbled backward. Had I been wearing his hiking boots I undoubtedly would have shattered his kneecap, but with my black dress loafers the kick only slowed him down. I scrambled to my feet awkwardly—hands behind the back tend to throw off your balance—and I lunged forward and swung my leg all the way back and kicked him in the stomach. He went down, but unfortunately the effort sent me sprawling, too. I got to my feet the same time he did. He was limping and looked very put out.

"Damn it, Saxon, you can't win. You're tied." His hand shot out and caught me under the eye, and his knuckles were hard. I fell backward and sat down again, this time going all the way back on my hands, and even before I had time to sit up again I felt my cheek puffing and swelling. I rolled over and got on my knees and he clubbed me on the back of the head and sent me flat on my face again, and it hurt so much all I wanted to do was to slip peacefully back to sleep so that the hurting would stop, but there was some bulldog inside me snarling at me to get up, to fight, to buy even a few more seconds of life, and I managed to get one knee under me and when he came at me again I butted him in the crotch with my head. He grunted and doubled over but, trussed up as I was, I couldn't take advantage of the moment, so I had to scramble around on the ground like a crippled animal, trying to get to my feet, and by that time he had sufficiently recovered to pull me up and hit me in the face again, and this time I did lose all sense of time and place for a second or two. When I opened my eyes I was lying on my back in the dirt and there was very little breath or fight left in me, and I was aware of noise and motion just above me and to my right, and when I was able to focus I saw that Buck Weldon had come out of nowhere and was charging Kullander, his blackthorn walking stick held like a Louisville Slugger, and then he swung it, one of those picture-book, Reggie Jackson–type swings from the heels, and it connected with Kullander's breastbone, and the stick snapped with almost as loud a crack as did the bone it hit, and Kullander screamed and went to one knee and then Buck Weldon was all over him, fists hammering like pistons, knees pumping and connecting, and he grabbed one of Kullander's ears and wrenched, and the ear came partly away from the skull with a spurt of blood and another bellow of anguish from Kullander, and then the two of them were rolling around on the ground, Kullander six inches taller and thirty pounds heavier and twenty years younger, and Buck was just whaling the kapok out of him, butting and kicking and gouging, and then the weight began to tell and Kullander was on top of him, his knees pinning Buck's chest and his long, strong fingers wrapped around his throat. His arms were a lot longer than Buck's so that Buck couldn't get to his face. I tried to stand but I was just too beaten up and I couldn't seem to get a purchase to get to my feet, and then all at once Buck's flailing hand found one of the rocks lying all over the ground and his fingers, blunt and calloused, closed around it. His first blow pulverized Kullander's elbow and made him let go of Buck's throat, and the second one crashed against Kullander's temple. The fight was over.

And so was the Buck Weldon case.

○ **14** ○

When I finally limped back to the cabin with Buck, whose insomnia had saved both our lives, we proceeded to get very drunk, and I didn't even care that I was drinking bourbon. We went at it with intoxication in mind, that single-mindedness of the serious drinker. This was to be no evening of social quaffing, of clinking glasses and swapping stories about beautiful women or no-hit baseball games that we'd seen or the funny things our platoon sergeants had said back in our army days. This was a night of heavy and hard boozing to help us come to terms with the fact that Buck had just killed a man and I had conspired to help him get away with it. Neither of us felt particularly proud of ourselves. It was something that was a necessary evil. The old Duke Wayne cliché about a man having to do what he had to do came to mind, but it wasn't much of a help. Buck Weldon and Bart Steele had finally blurred the fine lines of distinction between them; the Fascist Avenger had stepped off the pages of Buck Weldon's novels and into a quiet woodsy clearing in the mountains of Baja California, Mexico, and one of the Black Hats now lay dead and broken at the bottom of the same arroyo where he had planned to leave our bodies to molder into dust and time.

Eventually the hard drinking took its toll and I stood up and moved unsteadily into the bathroom to relieve myself, and when I had done so I caught a glimpse of the face in the mirror. My appearance qualified me to be chatting with Ferdie Pacheco at ringside and sending hello messages to my mother watching the fight at home. There was a cut over my eye, and the blood had run down over my cheekbone and chin where it had dried in an ugly red-brown streak; all along one side of my face was a vicious scrape made by Kullander's bootsole, and though there was some dried blood there too it was mostly just raw and red and angry-looking; the mouse under my eye had swelled up large enough to qualify for rathood. I was a mess.

In the morning we were both suffering from the troll king of hangovers, mine even more severe than his because I was less used to marathon drinking. Buck made some strong, bad coffee and after we'd killed a pot of it I found Bo Kullander's car and, with Buck following, drove it a hundred miles down the peninsula, taking care to wear a pair of hiking gloves so as not to leave any fingerprints. I left it parked just off the roadway, and then Buck picked me up in his Jeep and we drove back to Bonita. The Baja road had a well-earned reputation for attracting nomadic gangs of bandits, and I figured it wouldn't be an hour before the car had either disappeared or been stripped of so many parts as to make it virtually unidentifiable. We did have the foresight, however, to remove the California license plates, which, some fifty miles north of where we'd abandoned the car, I carelessly buried in a ditch.

At the hotel in Bonita I made a few phone calls. The first was to Jo, to let her know that I was all right.

"Who was it?" she said.

"Don't ask, Jo. Don't ever ask me about the case. As a matter of fact, I want you to take the Weldon file and all the notes and burn them. Other than the fact that Buck Weldon is a famous author and your boss dated his daughter a few times, you never heard of him."

"I've never burned a file before," she said.

"There have been a lot of firsts about this case, Jo. But I gave my word, and you have to do what I say."

There was a hurt silence. Then she said, "You can tell *me*, can't you? After all, it was my husband's almost getting shot that started this whole business." Her voice was like a little girl's.

I thought for a moment and said, "All I can tell you is this, honey. Marsh was right. It was the Mafia."

After I hung up I negotiated with the Mexican operator and finally got through to my own number in Pacific Palisades. After a few rings Valerie Weldon answered the phone.

"Hey, this is a neat place you've got here," she said. "Except your records suck. Don't you have any rock and roll?"

"What's the matter with Lawrence Welk?" I demanded.

"When are you coming home? I'm getting lonesome." Apparently Abdul Muhammad's death hadn't slowed her down even a step.

"Let me talk to your sister."

An exasperated sigh, then, "All right, if you're into neurotic feedback."

I heard the receiver clunk onto the table and after a few moments Tori said "Hello," very low and guarded and almost unbearably appealing, and I felt that little quickening that happened inside me whenever I heard her voice or saw her face.

"You can go home now," I said. "If you want to."

"My God, I've been frantic. I've been hysterical for two days. Where are you?"

"I'm all right," I said, fingering my butchered face. "And Buck is all right. And he will be, too. It's all over."

She didn't say anything for a moment and from the way she was breathing I could tell she was crying.

162

"It's all right, Peanut," I said, "there's no more danger. Save those tears until you can cry them on my shoulder. Okay?"

She sniffled a bit. It was cute.

We chatted a few minutes more, with her asking direct questions and me being evasive, and then when our conversation was over, I said softly, "I love you, Peanut."

She didn't answer me.

I hung up, but Tori and I were not quite finished, yet. I wondered if she would give me the chance to complete what we'd started, or at least to give it a try. I hoped so. I hoped that I'd have the opportunity of getting rid of the strange and wonderful granny knot she'd tied in my stomach.

Buck drove me to the airport in his Jeep that evening. He had decided to stay in Los Santos a few more days and sort things out in his mind. As we walked through the little terminal he said, "And I've got your word about you-know-what?"

"You've got it, Buck. But I wish you'd change your mind. I think it's time you did that. Come out of the closet and take the cheers you have coming to you."

At the foot of the steps to the plane on the runway he clapped me on the back. "Thanks is kind of a pussy word after what you've done for me," he said. "You're a good man, and I just want you to know that if you want to call on Tori, well, you have my permission."

I started to laugh and then I saw that he was serious. "I appreciate that, Buck, I really do. You'll be seeing me around. I hang in there."

"I've seen that."

I started up the steps and then he stopped me. His grin split his face but his eyes were glittering with pride and emotion. "I *am* as tough as Bart Steele, God damn it. All these years I wondered. But I really am."

"Buck," I told him, "there was never any question."

The flight up to Los Angeles seemed endless, and I was tired in every bone and muscle, more tired still in my brain. It was the beginning of Christmas vacation, and Bo Kullander wouldn't be missed at school for at least another two weeks. As for his friends, it was hard to say. I wondered if he'd been invited someplace for Christmas dinner or whether he'd had a date for New Year's Eve. In any event he would probably be listed as one of the many people who simply disappear each year without a trace. If the Mexican officials did find and identify him, there would be no way they could or would link him with me or with Buck Weldon. And the Los Angeles police were unlikely to ask too many questions about a body found in the hills of Mexico, either. They had enough troubles in their own jurisdiction. And if they, if Lieutenant Jamie Douglas or Joe DiMattia ever got around to cracking the Shelley Gardner murder, they could very neatly blame it on Abdul Muhammad, who was dead and wouldn't care one way or the other. Abdul's own death would be written off as person or persons unknown and the whole thing would be forgotten within six months.

So everyone was in the clear except me. I had a bad, perhaps terminal case of green eyes and pouty lips and blond angel hair.

Inside my apartment it was almost as though the Weldon sisters had never been there. Whatever dishes and glassware they had used had been washed and put away, there were clean sheets on the bed, and the towels (and some dirty clothes of mine) had been laundered and folded. There was a note on the dining room table, but all it said was, "Thanks. Tori," in that little-girl scrawl with the big circle over the "i."

I went to my message machine, whose light was blinking crazily. I rewound it and put it in the playback mode and poured myself a Laphroaig while I listened.

Beep!

Ray Tucek's raspy voice. "Hey, it's Ray. Let a guy know what's going down, all right? I'm worried about you. You still owe me some money."

Good old Ray. That's what friends are all about. He didn't give a damn about the money, he *was* worried about me. I wished that some day I could tell him exactly what he'd been involved in, but that was up to Buck. One thing I could never tell him, or anyone, and that was about Kullander and the arroyo. That was one I'd have to check out with.

Beep!

My agent: "Got a reading for you over at Lorimar if you get back to me within the next three hours. Otherwise, forget it."

Easy come, easy go. There would be other readings at Lorimar. Or maybe not. But there are priorities.

Beep!

A woman's voice, all too familiar, and for a moment it made me jump. "It's Leila. How are you? I miss seeing you. Call me and maybe we can have lunch during the holidays. Bye, sweetie."

I stopped the machine for a moment to examine how I was feeling about that one. Leila would have to have lunch with her broker friend. That was a closed chapter in the Book of Saxon. Of course perhaps she just wanted to be friends—well, maybe we could go out for a few drinks and pick up some girls. I did that with my friends sometimes.

After I'd had a few hits off the Scotch I started the machine up again.

Beep!

Bill Laven: "Hello, there. Haven't heard from you in a while and was just wondering if all is calm, all is bright. Call me."

Dear Bill, my die-hard Chicagoan and unregenerated Cub fan who lived in Los Angeles for the climate but whose heart was firmly rooted on the Chicago lakefront. The message he'd left on my tape was probably the shortest speech he'd ever made in his life.

Beep!

A reedy, misleadingly soft Godfather voice: "DiMattia here. Call me!"

Not tonight, Joseph. I'm not up to it. Maybe tomorrow. Not tonight.

Beep!

And then that low, guarded, musical voice that got me up out of my chair, the voice I'd been hearing inside my head since the first time it had said hello: "It's Tori." Long pause, and then with a sincerity that made my head ring, "I love you, too."

My gaze went around the room to my ficus plant, and I noticed that near the base of one of the browning, withered branches there was a tiny little green bud just beginning to show. Not much, not enough to make me quit worrying about it, not really enough to take it off the critical list. But something.

Hope.